Haze

Kathy Hoopmann

Jessica Kingsley Publishers
London and Philadelphia

First published in the United Kingdom in 2003
by Jessica Kingsley Publishers
116 Pentonville Road
London N1 9JB, UK
and
400 Market Street, Suite 400
Philadelphia, PA 19106, USA

www.jkp.com

Copyright © Kathy Hoopmann 2003
Printed digitally since 2009

Library of Congress Cataloging in Publication Data
A CIP catalog record for this book is available from the Library of Congress

British Library Cataloguing in Publication Data
A CIP catalogue record for this book is available from the British Library

ISB 978 1 84310 072 0

Contents

For Kay Bridges
A friend since forever

Acknowledgements

With many thanks to Tony Attwood, Daniel Tullemans and Helena Bond for help with the manuscript. Also my deepest gratitude to Tim Schier for his expert computer advice. Any inaccuracies are mine alone.

The author gratefully acknowledges that *Haze* was written with the help of the Arts Queensland grant.

Chapter 1

Seb

I

Seb lay on the trampoline in his sleeping bag, a pillow tucked under his head. Set for the night, he gently bounced his body through the pressure of his feet. Backforwardbackforwardbackforward. The rhythm calmed his body a little, but his mind churned. He watched the stars and relived the evening.

It had been the night of The School Dance. His mother said he had to go. "Just for a little while, Seb," she pleaded, "Get away from the computer for a couple of hours."

"It'll be great," Dad said. "A chance to meet some girls."

He hadn't seen the way kids dance these days. Bodies melded together, knowing the moves. The moves hidden from teachers. The moves nobody taught Seb.

From the second Seb had entered the hall he knew it was a mistake. There were too many people. Too much noise. The music blared. Lights flashed. Smells of sweat and banned substances. If it wasn't for Guzzle, his friend since forever, he would have left immediately.

"Come on," Guzzle urged. "Give it a go."

Seb stood at the back a long time and observed. He tried to work out the rules, but gave up. It was all too hard. Then he saw Kristie. A girl from his class. One of the few who ever said hi. With his stomach churning, he asked her, "Would you like to dance?" Mistook her grimace for a smile. She was too polite to say no. He didn't know the difference. Danced awkwardly facing each other for one interminable song and then she was gone.

"Stupid nerd," Guzzle yelled later over the music. "She can't stand ya. Can't ya tell?"

Seb couldn't think. "No. How can you tell?" he asked, feeling stupid…again. He knew the feeling well.

"See the way she looked back at her friends and scrunched up her face. That says she didn't wanna to dance with ya."

Seb stared into the darkness. Bounce, bounce on the cold black mat.

The stars flickered. Dying suns and asteroids choreographed their own dance in the sky. And Seb watched, separated from the cosmic display by eons of time and space vacuum.

Like my life, Seb thought. There's a world out there I know nothing about. A crazy stream of data that bombards every waking minute of every day.

Seb's rocking became more vigorous. His back moulded to the firm matting. He tried to thrust away the haze through which he saw life, that warped his perceptions and confused his mind.

Rocked on and on into the night, getting nowhere.

II

"How was the dance?" Seb's mother asked warily over breakfast. A night on the trampoline was a warning that things were not well with her son.

"I would have preferred to have read the dictionary."

Mrs Taylor knew Seb was not joking. For a start he never joked. Well, that wasn't quite true. He had his own sense of humour no one else quite understood. And secondly he'd been reading the dictionary every night for a while now. Before that, he'd read the encyclopaedia and the thesaurus.

"Did you get to dance? Meet anyone new?"

"Yes and no." Seb got up from the table and walked away. Conversation over.

She bit her lip and did not call him back. No point. That had been their longest chat in days.

Seb walked to school. He could have caught a bus, but loathed the clamour. Always had to stand because no one would share a seat. Besides he liked the thud of his feet on the concrete path. Trod heavily for extra rhythm. Thumped fence posts as he went. Never stopped for anything. But he slowed as he neared the school gates and readied himself for the day.

Breath came faster.

Throat dry. Knew the signs.

Could tick them off like a check list.

Everything stiffened…neck, arms, groin. Nails dug into soft palm flesh, tearing at the ever-present scabs.

It was almost a relief when school came in sight and he saw them waiting at the gate. Standing where they usually did once or twice a week ever since the beginning of the year, day one.

How did they know that he was an easy target? As if an aura followed him everywhere that cried, 'I am a victim. Torment me.'

"The first three letters in **Dan**gerous and don't you forget it," was how Dan introduced himself, after he'd spat at Seb that first day.

Chalk. Tall and thin and white. Pale of skin, pale of eyes, pale of mind.

And Kaziah. Her beauty hid the dark creature that she really was. Clever too. Got good grades. Behaved in class. Teachers never believed a bad word about her. Why would they?

Dan. Kaziah. Chalk.

Seb knew he was not their only target.

But it didn't help when Dan and Chalk tripped him and pushed him and tore his clothes and Kaziah watched, sleek, like a cat.

And once they'd gone and he pushed himself to his feet, face bland, Seb raged at his inability to understand …why him?

III

There was a new teacher in Seb's computer class today. Younger than most. Still had hair in a ponytail. Probably her first year out.

Barely older than her students.

"I am Miss Adonia," she said. Her voice was soft and clear with the hint of an accent. The day was cool so the fans were not clacking. One less thing for Seb to cope with.

The fluorescent lights flickered though, as usual, so he pulled his hat lower over his eyes expecting to be told to remove it. Miss Adonia did not notice. Or if she did, she did not care.

She read the roll, closed the book then smiled and repeated everyone's name. Seb was not impressed. He could do that. Knew the periodic table by heart. Lists were easy.

It was people who were hard.

Kristie, the girl who danced with him last night, the girl who taught him about grimaces, called out, "Good memory, Miss." It was just a comment, but Kaziah glanced across the room at Kristie. Looked at her with slit eyes beneath long lashes.

Hungry eyes.

Kaziah did not like competition in class. Seb knew Kristie would have a bad time today. He knew it because he had learned the long lash look. Taught himself the meaning. Had lots of experience.

Miss Adonia may have been young, but she knew computers. Mr Roberts, their usual teacher, was sick, she said, and would be away for some weeks. Seb sat up, pleased. Mr Roberts was old. Close to retirement. Seb knew much more about computers than Mr Roberts. More than most teachers, actually. Mr Roberts did not like to be corrected in front of his class and Seb spent many lessons at the office for impertinence.

Maybe Miss Adonia knew things that Seb did not know.

That would be rare.

That would be good.

IV

Lunch times were the worst. No structure. Bored teachers begrudging supervising duties. Seb had his own routine. When Guzzle was at footy training, or cricket practice or basketball training, like most days, Seb sat alone under the buildings to eat. Near the crowd so he could listen — listen to other people's lives. At a glance it seemed as if he had friends.

He didn't sit too close.

Never too close. Learnt that one early. Had bruises for a week to help. Kids you don't know, don't like to have their invisible circle infiltrated.

By nerds.

By gaybos.

By geeks.

Seb was none of those, but did not have the words to explain his worth to others.

Lunch was always a ham roll and chocolate milk. "That will be four fifty-five," he echoed the canteen lady under his breath.

Then Seb headed for the library. To the safety of silence and the solidarity of facts.

He heard Kaziah's voice before he saw her. The low purr triggered the flight reflex in his brain. His head jerked. Fear made Seb a poorly controlled puppet.

Glossy hair flicked in a parting in the crowd.

Seb sighed in relief. He was not her target this time.

Then he saw. This time it was Kristie. Kristie... who danced with him even when she didn't have to. Kristie with face full of fear, and marble-still eyes.

"Leave her alone," he heard his voice say. How had he moved so fast? Kaziah turned with feline grace, her tongue flicked over slick wet lips.

"Well, if it's not Sebastian Taylor," she hissed. Liquid menace poured over him.

"Leave her alone," Seb's voice repeated, as he stared at his feet.

"Didn't know you had a girlfriend," Kaziah's words slid from her throat. "Thought you didn't like *girls*, full stop." She ran a finger down Seb's cheek. Flesh twitched. He slapped at her hand.

"Touchy," she laughed.

A teacher walked past uninterested, but Kaziah backed away.

"Later," she said.

Seb did not look up.

Did not know to whom she spoke.

Did not see the look on Kristie's face as she looked at Seb.

Would not have known what it meant anyway.

Even Kristie did not know.

Seb went to the library and stared at a computer screen.

Chapter 2

Madeline, Kristie and Jen

I

There was not much that Madeline missed through the veil of her fringe. Her personal burqa. The daily play of banter and taunts had a silent audience.

She watched a gaggle of girls around the picnic tables eating sausage rolls, dripping sauce onto crisp white paper bags. They asserted their individuality by copying trends. Butterfly clips this week. Butterflies in braids, in pigtails carelessly caught, in looped under coils and in untameable ringlets. Butterflies in perms and streaks and undercuts and plaits.

Boys sauntered by with hats on back to front and oversized jerseys hiding soft fuzz body hair.

Madeline knew that not only cigarettes were smoked behind the toilets. Knew those who went without, scavenging tossed sandwiches when no one was looking. Knew who really ran the school, and it wasn't the teachers. Knew that Dan and Chalk constantly feared being upstaged; that Kaziah was not the prettiest girl.

She saw the ebb and flow of school ground politics, the flotsam it left in some people's lives. She beachcombed the gossip, the lies, the hurts, the rumours and occasionally, just occasionally, saw a surface splash that hinted at something deeper.

Today, the riptide was Seb. Madeline had noticed Seb before. Brilliant with numbers and facts. Hopeless with people.

Why did he challenge Kaz? Did he understand what he had done? Probably not.

Madeline rose from her back corner and walked unseen through the crowd. It parted for her as she knew it would. The ultimate invisible person. It had taken years to cultivate, this air of insubstantiality. Her face was set with a hint of a smile. Pleasant, people would say. If anyone had cared enough to notice, they would think she was heading for a friend. Walk firmly, with purpose, even when there was nowhere to go. She followed Seb to the library and sat a long way behind him.

And watched.

II

"I told you I could," Seb said.

Guzzle had finished training and found Seb in the library, in the room set aside for student computer access. The computers were never meant for half the things they were used for.

Guzzle stared at the screen, eyes wide. "Shit," he whispered so the librarian wouldn't hear. "Are they really the teachers' passwords?"

"Yeah."

"And ya can change them if ya want?"

"Yeah."

"Shit."

"That's a good one," Seb grinned. "We could change Miss Adonia's password to 'shit'."

"Your new computer teacher?"

"Yeah."

"Go on. Do it."

"Nah. Wouldn't be right."

"I dare ya."

Seb scrolled down the screen. "Miss Adonia doesn't have an account yet."

He scrolled again. "Must have used Mr Roberts'."

"Someone else then. Barbarella." The principal.

Seb hesitated. "Better not. I'm the only kid in the school who can do this. They'd find out it was me for sure."

"Modest aren't ya."

"It's the truth."

"Can ya change grades too? Give me straight 'A's."

"I can, but I won't. I'm just in here to look."

"Come on," Guzzle urged. "What about me 'F's? Could ya change a fail to a C minus? No one would care. It wouldn't hurt anyone."

"But they're last term's results. They've already been sent out."

Guzzle grinned. "I threw the letter in the bin. Mum doesn't know. If ya change them now she never will. It'll make her proud if I pass."

Seb nodded. That was fair enough.

He went into a different file. It only took a minute. Guzzle's report now had straight 'C's, except for PE. He got an 'A' for physical education all by himself.

"Sweet." Guzzle grinned. "Now yours."

Seb brought his grades onto the screen. 'A' for advanced maths, and computer studies. Nothing else mattered.

"I'll leave them," he said.

III

The phone rang.

Seb's dad raised his eyebrows as he handed across the receiver. "It's a girl!" he said too loudly.

Seb put the phone to his ear and waited.

"Seb?"

"Yeah."

Seb's father read his newspaper, but Seb knew he was still listening.

"It's Kristie."

Kristie of the grimace. "Yeah?"

"I, um, just wanted to say thanks. You know, for sticking up for me today. Against Kaz."

"Yeah?" Why did he say that? That was stupid. Seb gulped. What was he supposed to say?

There was silence.

It yawned and swallowed them both.

"Well, I'd better go," Kristie said quickly. "Just wanted to say thanks."

"OK." Seb hung up.

It had gone badly.

Incredibly badly.

Seb did not look his father's way. Did not want to see the pain in his father's eyes. Didn't need to – he could look in a mirror for that. Seb had failed again. Failed to talk normally to a girl.

'Just add it to the list, Dad,' Seb raged inside.

He went to his room and shut the door.

The computer beckoned him with comforting cathode rays.

IV

"I feel so stupid. Why did I phone him?" Kristie moaned into her mobile.

"Because, chicky babe, beneath that ugly mug you have a heart of gold," Jen suggested. She curled under a blanket, the receiver to her ear.

Jen was Kristie's friend. New to the school this year. She hung around with Kaz for a while 'til she got stung once too often.

"But he said nothing. It was like I was talking to a zombie."

"Confucius say, 'Beneath every zombie is life to be revealed,'" Jen said in a clipped voice.

"Up Confucius. What do I do now?"

"Do? Stay away from Kaz."

"I mean about Seb. How can I face him tomorrow?"

"I don't think you'll have to face him. Poor guy. He'll probably run a mile if he sees *you*."

"Good."

"Really? I thought you liked him. You even danced with him. I saw."

"It's hard to like someone who won't talk to you. And he dances like a jerk. Literally. All twitches and judders."

"Maybe he needs private lessons," Jen hinted.

"Not from me."

"Come on. Admit you like him. You must or you wouldn't have rung him."

"I only wanted to say thanks."

"Sure, babe."

"Jen!"

"Why not ask him to help you with your chemistry homework? That'd get him talking."

"You think?"

"Might stir up the chemistry between you anyway!"

"Get lost! I'm going to bed."

SEB PLAYED A mindless game on the computer and tried to forget Kristie. Lost track of time. Stared at the phone for 27 minutes and 38 seconds before he gained enough courage.

He dialled Kristie's number.

A man's voice, full of sleep, groaned, "Goddam. Who the hell is this? It's nearly midnight."

Seb hung up, heart thumping.

Breathing hard, he picked at the scabs on his hands.

V

"What do you think, Seb?"

Seb flicked a glance at Miss Adonia. Had no idea what she was talking about. Couldn't sleep last night. Or eat this morning. He refused to acknowledge Kristie at the far computer station. Everything was out of kilter. The haze was heavy today.

"About hacking. Do hackers always leave their mark or can they break into computer systems without a trace?" Miss Adonia prompted.

Seb blinked. He did not want to participate. The joy of computer studies was that he did not have to listen to teacher talk. Just him off with the pixels.

"Crackers," he said finally.

Miss Adonia understood immediately. "Very good, Seb." She turned to the class. "Seb is right, hackers design programs. They're purists. Crackers are what we're really talking about, those who break into others' programs illegally. But for the sake of the uneducated masses, we'll call them hackers. Can you trace them?" she prompted Seb.

Seb shrugged. "Maybe."

"Could you be more specific?"

Seb breathed deep, interested despite himself. "They usually leave a trace, but there are ways of covering themselves – then they're almost impossible to track."

"Ahh, but would the average hacker bother?" Miss Adonia pressed her hands together like she was praying and bought fingertips to her lips. Eyes shone. She was enjoying this. She continued in her own stream of thought. "Surely they feel supreme. Sitting in dingy offices and home studies, at Internet cafes and at coffee stained desks. Yet they roam the world. Influence world events!" She flung her hands into the air like an actress. "Such power at fingertips, …literally." She laughed at her own joke. "Why bother to hide? Perhaps hackers want to be caught so they can tell the world how clever they are?"

Kristie raised her hand. "Maybe they have their own agenda," she said. "Maybe they get their kicks out of keeping things to themselves. Some people are like that." She stared hard at Miss Adonia so her eyes would not seek out Seb.

"The Scarlet Pimpernel," Kaziah said softly.

Miss Adonia smiled in delight. "We seek him here, we seek him there. Those Frenchies seek him everywhere!"

she quoted. "Excellent, Kaziah. He had the need to be recognised, but not to be found. The perfect hacker."

"So you gonna teach us how to hack, Miss?" one kid called out.

"Yeah, transfer a million bucks into my account?"

"Download porn without paying!"

In reply, Miss Adonia's hands flittered across the central computer and the screens came alive in front of each student.

She ignored the groans as statistics scrolled up. "Bar graphs, class. Beauty in rectangles with attitude. Enjoy!"

Seb set to work. At last a domain in which he felt secure.

And as he entered the final information, a message flashed across his screen.

"Hello, Mr Pimpernel."

Chapter 3

Sleepover

I

"Kristie, do you know a girl at school named Madeline Story? She's about your age," Kristie's mum asked as she made dinner.

"Yeah. She's in a couple of my classes. Why?"

"She's staying here on Friday night."

"What!"

"Her mother works with me at the bank. She has no family close. She has to attend an overnight seminar on the coast and seemed a bit desperate so I said Madeline could stay with us."

Madeline Story.

Tall…brown hair…quiet. That was it. That was all Kristie knew about a girl she had spent years criss-crossing paths with. Like threads on a loom finally drawn to meet.

"Can Jen stay over too?"

"If you like."

"MADELINE STORY? WHICH one is she?" Jen peered round the grounds.

"Can't see her. Sits by herself. Never says anything."

"Short hair that's always in her eyes?"

"Yeah, that's her."

MADELINE WATCHED THEM from behind a trellis screen, and was afraid.

Afraid that they were exactly the type of girls she would choose as friends.

If she wanted friends.

And she didn't.

Across the quadrangle where students mingled and ate, Miss Adonia sat next to Seb. Madeline blinked. It was like looking at a children's book. 'Spot what's wrong with this picture.' Teachers don't sit next to students. They stand and command. They can be pleasant and helpful, but they never sit.

Seb stared at the concrete. Shuffled his feet. Then Miss Adonia stood and walked away. Seb headed straight for the library.

Madeline followed unnoticed, like a ghost.

II

Guzzle sat under the bridge and threw clods of dirt into what was left of the stream. He tried to hit water and not plastic bags, the odd needle and other garbage. It was a suburban bridge spanning a trickling brook. Had a footpath underneath so people could avoid the traffic. The stream would have been beautiful once. Maybe two hundred years ago. Clean and pure and pretty with bird calls and snuffling animals.

Guzzle took a can of spray paint from his bag and tagged the concrete pylon. TWS. With a spiral twist ending. The World Sucks. Better not tell Seb. He had this weird fixation about obeying rules. At least, now, there was something worth looking at. Guzzle's persona for all to see.

He glanced at his watch: 11am. Recess at school. He took out a bun from his bag. Unwrapped it and tossed the plastic film onto the breeze. An enormous transparent butterfly.

Guzzle *had* to skip school this morning. The ancient history assignment was due. Who cared about ancient freakin' history? Only took the stupid subject because the other choices were worse. Besides he knew all about ancient history. Watched every episode of Xena, Warrior

Princess. Knew that Hercules was Zeus's bastard son. Liked the thought that a bastard could rise to such heights. Was a bastard himself. His step dad, Angus, never let him forget it. Guzzle called him Anus, but never to his face. But this assignment was not about Greece. It was an analysis of the balance of power in the 15th century. And it was not finished.

Get real.

It was not even started.

Can't go to school til lunch, Guzzle thought. Don't wanna miss sport.

Across the road was a small shopping centre. There was a cafe called Lucky Joes with outdoor tables where kids met after school. Made great fries. Beside it were a newsagent, a bakery and a real estate agent. From under the bridge Guzzle watched as people ate and chatted, mums mainly, with little kids hanging off their arms, begging for ice-cream.

A teenager with a ponytail looked at a community noticeboard which advertised local businesses. An older man stood beside her. Her father? What were they seeking? Maybe they wanted a pet. Perhaps a place to stay.

The girl turned and Guzzle grunted in surprise. It was Miss Adonia, Seb's new teacher. He'd never thought of teachers existing outside school. Wouldn't have been surprised if they had computer chips in their brains that turned off at 3pm when kids went home and only reset at 9 the next morning.

The man casually touched Miss Adonia's waist and ushered her into Lucky Joes. She flinched and stared warily at him.

No love lost there, Guzzle thought. He shrugged and looked away. Wasn't his worry. Had enough worries of his own.

III

"Mr Pimpernel? She called ya that?" Guzzle asked, a burger half way to his mouth.

"Who else could it have been? Miss Adonia's the only one who has that sort of computer knowledge," Seb said toying with his milk shake.

"So she knows. Shit, I'll get me 'F's back."

"Maybe not. At lunch she asked my opinion about the new stand alone computers the school's just bought and she never mentioned you at all."

"What did she ask ya that for?"

"I probably impressed her in class. I told her what we were getting. They're the latest Pentiums. Do you have any idea how much power those things have?"

"Nah." Guzzle watched little kids crawl over the playground outside the cafe. Seb's voice droned on about bits and bytes. Didn't need any response from Guzzle to keep momentum. A perpetual machine. One jab and it goes forever. Seb had always been like that. Could talk non stop about whatever interested him.

"I saw her today. Miss Adonia," Guzzle said suddenly. Seb stopped mid sentence. "At morning tea. She musta left school for a bit. She came in here."

"Did you skip school again?" The disapproval in Seb's voice made Guzzle wince. Seb of contrasts. Brains of a bloody rocket scientist. Morals of an old lady.

"Not much. She was with a man. Old enough to be her dad."

Seb nodded. Her dad. He thought of Kristie's dad. How angry he sounded last night.

"She hates me," Seb said sadly.

"What? Miss Adonia? Why?" Guzzle asked, confused.

"No, Kristie. She rang me and I acted like a jerk."

"What's new?" Guzzle laughed, then stopped suddenly at the look on Seb's face. "It was a joke, mate. A joke. So Kristie rang ya. Sweet. She must really like ya."

"What makes you say that?"

"Well she danced with ya didn't she, and now she's phonin' ya up. Go for it mate."

"But she didn't want to dance with me. You said."

"Yeah, but she rang ya. That changes things. Ask her for a date."

Seb broke out in a sweat, and his hand shook as he slid the last of his drink into his mouth. Holding hands. Kissing. Talking, just the two of them. Touching. How do you do that? Any of it.

"Relax, mate. There's nothing to it. Go to the movies or something. You don't have to talk and if she lets ya, you can touch her up in the dark."

"Touch her up? What does that mean?"

"Geez mate. Grab her boobs."

Seb felt sick. Guzzle made it sound so easy. So natural. He always had girlfriends. But then Guzzle was six foot three, fit and good looking. Had his pick of football groupies. Seb was tall too, but scrawny. Never one for sports. Walked stooped in an attempt to hide from the world.

The only reason they were friends was that they'd met before looks counted. Before sport defined a man. Before others decided that Seb was a nerd and not worth bothering with. Seb was loyal and honest. That was enough for Guzzle. Seb was a stability in a shifting life that was full of let downs.

"Listen mate," Guzzle said gently seeing Seb's distress. "Just hold her hand. Tell her she's pretty. That'll do for starters."

Hold her hand. Fingers to fingers. He could do that.

Sure. He could do that.

IV

The remains of the pizza lay at the bottom of the box. The oil that oozed from the crust left a perfect circle on the cardboard. Kristie and Jen sprawled on the lounge floor. Madeline sat cross legged, arms casually folded. She felt dangerously relaxed and almost happy. It was the first time she had ever slept away from her mother. It was as if she'd lived a life time in a cloud and had finally peeked at the sun.

Mother would have some way of spoiling it later.

Would twist things.

Pervert them.

It was what she did best.

"*Candid Cards?*" Kristie asked, looking to the others for approval.

"Great!" Jen agreed.

"It's a game," Kristie said, seeing Madeline's puzzled look as she pulled a box from a cupboard. "A game of questions. You pick a card and we ask you a question. You answer. We have to guess if you're telling the truth or a lie."

Madeline froze. Her life was built on secrecy. Not that there was anything to hide. But Mother disliked 'loose tongues'.

"You first," Jen said offering the cards to Kristie. Kristie cut the pack and the top card read SCHOOL'S COOL.

Jen picked it up and read, "Did you ever cheat on a test?"

"Who me?" Kristie cooed. "Never."

"What? Not once? Ever? Not even a little peek in spelling tests?"

"No."

"Liar!" Jen laughed. "What do you think, Maddy?"

Madeline squirmed. She didn't want to play. Dreaded her turn.

"Do you think she's ever cheated or not?"

Madeline nodded reluctantly. "Probably."

"So. Are we right? Have you cheated?"

"Well, maybe once. When I was very young," Kristie conceded.

"Yes!" Jen punched the air. "A point to you and me, Maddy."

Madeline was about to correct her, to say her name was Madeline, but stopped. Realised she didn't mind.

Jen selected a card. BODY BLUES. She groaned.

"What part of your body do you dislike the most?" Kristie read.

All of it, Madeline answered silently to herself.

"None of it," Jen said proudly. "I'm perfect."

"Liar!" Kristie shouted. She mimicked Jen's voice. "My breasts are too small. I'm too fat. My hair's a mess."

Jen threw a pillow at her.

"Maddy's turn," Kristie said.

With heavy fingers Madeline took a card from the pack. BABY DAYS.

Baby days. What was that? Playing? Fun times? Freedom? …not.

"Did you ever have a make believe friend?"

Madeline tensed. Why that question? It touched a place no one had ever been. Not even her mother. Especially not Mother.

"Well?" Jen prompted.

"Yes," Madeline said. She swallowed.

"Tell us more."

"Mr Minty. His name was Mr Minty."

"Maddy and Mr Minty. Cute," Kristie laughed. "I bet you blamed everything on him. It wasn't my fault. Mr Minty did it."

Madeline cringed inwardly. It was so far from the truth it sounded like blasphemy. Mr Minty who was always there for her, day or night. Who never let her down. More of a lifeline than an imaginary friend.

Madeline forced her lips to grin. "Things we do when we're young," she said.

"I believe you," Jen said.

"Me too," said Kristie.

Then Kristie's mum brought in dessert. A release just before too much was revealed. The game was abandoned in favour of ice-cream and cake, and Madeline smiled her thanks pleasantly and ate listening to the others' chatter.

Chapter 4

Rituals

I

Seb followed the same ritual every morning. Woke with the alarm at 6.30. Lay in bed until 6.34. Showered, dressed and had breakfast by 6.59. That was important. It all had to be done by then. If he was even one minute late then the rest of the day was unbearable. Tilted. Out of focus.

Once, Guzzle slept over and moved every clock in the house forward five minutes as a joke. Even though they were great friends, there were times when Guzzle couldn't resist upsetting Seb. Seb was so easy to annoy. Move his toothbrush to the other side of the basin. Sit on his chair. Change the order of his Star Trek magazines, filed chronologically. Six years of them. Not one missing or damaged.

There were three patched holes in the walls in Seb's room. It was the wall or Guzzle, and Seb, even in his darkest moments, managed to deflect his rage from flesh to plaster.

But this morning, his parents were the problem.

They were sitting at the table. Waiting.

"Seb, we need to talk," Mum said.

Seb glanced at his watch. 6.49am. He reached for the cereal box.

"Leave it, Seb. Have it later." His dad moved the box away. Seb stared at it, refusing to look at his parents.

"Dad and I are worried about you, Seb," Mum said. She went to stroke his arm. To let him know worry came from love, but he drew back.

"We think you might need some help."

"Help with what?" He spoke quickly, trying to speed up the conversation.

"With lots of things. With the problems you have getting along with people. With your unreasonable need for routine. With the bullying at school."

Seb stiffened. How did she know about that. He never told her.

"Who do you think repairs the rips in your clothes each week, Seb?" she answered his unasked question.

"We've booked you in to see the school counsellor, Seb," Dad said gruffly. "We're coming with you to see him on the first session, then after that you'll go on your own every Tuesday."

The school counsellor. Someone new. Asking questions. Seb's breathing quickened.

"We just want to help you, Seb. To see you happy."

"When?"

"The first appointment is tomorrow. Tuesday, 1pm."

"Lunch time?"

"Is that OK? We can change it if you like?"

The counsellor instead of library...on Tuesdays. Seb mentally logged it into his timetable. "It's OK," he said finally. It wasn't so bad, really. He could adapt given time. And maybe the counsellor could help. Maybe.

6.57am

Two minutes to eat breakfast.

The morning could be saved after all.

II

"There he is. Right on time," Dan grinned.

"Stupid geek. He knows we'll be here. Why doesn't he go through the other gate?" Chalk rolled grey eyes. "Some people deserve everything they get."

"What'll it be today? Grab the bag or the beat the bod?"

A smorgasbord to pick and choose.

"The bod. I feel like kickin' butt."

Seb rarely felt the kicks and punches. He had an extraordinarily high pain threshold. Once had a fractured arm for a week before his mother found out.

But he felt the humiliation. The futile anger. Couldn't understand why they hated him so much. Didn't know how to make them stop.

As he lay on the ground he realised they'd been quick today. 8.53am. Still time to get to class before the bell.

"Are you OK?"

Miss Adonia stood at the gate. She did not offer to help him up.

Where had she come from?

Seb glanced around. Chalk and Dan were walking towards the office with the principal, Mr Barbarella. Dan's shirt was ripped. Good.

"I had a tip-off you needed help. Someone added an appointment to my online schedule. Wonder how it got there?" Miss Adonia smiled.

Seb got to his feet, confused. "I didn't do it."

"Really? It wasn't you? Curious." She believed him instantly. Seb found it hard to read faces, but she showed no sign of sarcasm or doubt.

"Do you have any idea who can break into the school's servers…apart from yourself, of course?"

"I can't do that," Seb blushed.

"You're a rotten liar, Seb," Miss Adonia laughed. "People like you should stick to the truth."

"People like me? What do you mean?"

She ignored his question. "Do you know who could have hacked into my personal account?"

"No."

"Never mind. I'll find out. Sure you're OK?"

Seb nodded.

"See you in class then. Last period."

Seb watched her leave. The morning was all wrong. First his parents wanting to talk, then the principal catching Dan and Chalk in the act. Like jumping into a familiar stream only to find it flowing uphill. Seb bent down. Undid his shoelaces and retied them. Used the opportunity to shut his eyes. Shut out the world so that an inner calm could be restored. When he was a kid, he simply stood still, eyes squeezed tight, but age had given him techniques to hide his need.

Then he headed for class. 8.58am.

He should make it in time.

III

"Why don't you do your homework, Sebastian?" The counsellor leaned one elbow on the desk and supported his chin.

Seb stared at the floor.

His dad sat stony faced. His mother willed him to answer.

"You're a bright kid. You could get 'A's in every subject if you tried, not just maths and computer studies. Homework is compulsory. So you regularly fail a compulsory component of many subjects. Why?"

Because school is for schoolwork and home is for home things, Seb said to himself. Because I have to bust my brain every day coping with stupid rules and petty teachers and by the time I get home I want to veg out by myself for a while. To recharge.

"Dunno," Seb said.

The counsellor studied Seb's bowed head.

"Okaaay," he said slowly drawing out the sound. "Let's think positive for a while shall we?" He glanced at the notes on the desk. "Your computing skills are outstanding. Have you ever thought of taking advanced classes?"

"What do you mean?"

"After school. Some kids have afternoon sports training. You could have computer lessons."

Seb shrugged. Sounded all right.

"Would you agree to that?" the counsellor asked Seb's parents.

"Sounds wonderful," Mrs Taylor said.

"I'm all in favour of kids reaching their full potential and I'm well aware of the school's inability to provide opportunities for every need. Sometimes extra curricular is the way to go. In fact..." he shuffled through papers in his drawer, "...ahh, here it is. The new teacher, Miss Adonia, has offered to tutor kids interested in advanced programming. I could get her to call if you like?"

Seb nodded. Programming. His speciality. Doubted any teacher could tell much he didn't know, but it would be good to talk about it with someone who understood his language.

"Great!" the counsellor said. "We're getting somewhere. See you next Tuesday, Sebastian... and kid, try to do your homework."

Seb stood, walked to the door and opened it. "Kids are baby goats," he said as he went out.

IV

"No offence, Kristie, I just don't understand what you see in him," Jen said as they watched Seb come out of the counsellor's room. "I guess he is sort of good looking if you like that drawn face, dopey look. But he won't even talk to you."

"He's shy, that's all. Besides he's different from other guys."

"You can say that again."

"I mean, it's refreshing not have him come on to me like a walking testosterone time bomb."

"So you like him because he doesn't like you. Now who's weird?"

"I think he does like me. He just doesn't know how to show it."

"Prove it."

"What?"

"Go and talk to him now. See if he walks away. I dare you."

"OK. I will."

Kristie waited until Seb's mum and dad said their goodbyes. Seb slouched on the bench seat under the building and did not even look at them.

"I don't think he gets on with his parents too well," Kristie commented.

"He's a teenager. Ignoring his olds is the most normal thing I've seen him do," Jen said. "Now go and do your stuff, girl. Knock him dead."

And Jen watched as Kristie walked hesitantly over and sat next to Seb. Saw Seb's flicker of alarm and Kristie's quick smile.

And then they talked.

They actually talked.

Well, Seb talked to his shoes and Kristie listened intently…for a good thirty seconds.

Then she crossed her arms, bit a rough edge from a fingernail. Refused to catch Jen's eye.

Wriggled. Watched an ant walk up the wall. Wondered how it would carry a crumb so large. Picked fluff from her skirt. Finally she rose and Jen saw her say, "Thanks."

And as she slumped back next to Jen, Kristie said, "Remind me to *never* ask him advice about buying computers again."

V

"So you think he's the one?"

Miss Adonia sat on the small deck of their motel room contemplating the question. Stared at a tiny patch of night glazed lawn. A bizarre way to live. Surrounded by people you didn't know.

Secrets in boxes all in a row.

She turned back to the man on the couch. Rodin.

"Everything's pointing that way," she said. "Exceptional computing skills. A loner. Spends all his spare time on the library computers."

"Sounds promising."

"There's one thing that doesn't fit though," Miss Adonia said. "Someone added an appointment on my personal timetable to warn me that Seb was being bullied. No students have access to my account."

"It could have been him. It sounds like he has the talent."

"I know, but I don't think it was."

"Perhaps it was another teacher who wants the bullying stopped but doesn't want to do the hard work?"

Miss Adonia shrugged. "Maybe."

"So when will you be sure if Seb is our man?"

"I've arranged it so that I visit his house in two days."

"Good. Be careful what you say to him though. We don't want to tip him off early," Rodin said. "And in the meantime, keep your eyes open to the possibility he is *not* the one."

VI

"Guess what," Guzzle said as they wandered around the school ground after football training. "Miss Adonia is stayin' in that motel near the park. Ya can see her unit from the creek. I watched her last night sittin' on the deck with the old geezer."

"What were you doing in the park at night? Drinking again?"

"A bit. Gotta live up to me name, don't I?"

"Alcohol kills brain cells. You can't afford to lose any more."

"Hey! That's a joke. I don't believe it. Seb made a joke!"

"It wasn't a joke. It's the…"

"Yeah, yeah, I know. It's the truth. Anyway, thought you'd like to know."

"I went to the school counsellor yesterday."

"What?" Seb changed topics too fast for Guzzle.

"The school counsellor. With Mum and Dad."

"Geez mate. Why?"

"They think I'm psycho."

"All parents think their kids are psycho. What happened?"

"The counsellor knew everything about me. Had my reports back to when I was five."

"Shit."

"He said that I had to take more responsibility for my life. Told me I acted like a victim and therefore became one. Like it was my fault I got beaten up all the time. Even told Mum to buy me a new shirt so I fitted in better."

Guzzle said nothing. Seb had always dressed the same. Easy wear clothes, a size too large. Ripped the labels out so that the material frayed at the neck. Most of the things he wore were patched. Loved to death. That was Seb.

"He told me I had to show more respect to teachers. Even when I know they're wrong. Even when their rules are stupid."

"Bloody teachers."

"I have to see him every Tuesday to work through my…" Seb copied the counsellors voice, "*complex idiosyncrasies in social situations and the unusual contrast between victimisation at school and poor anger management at home.*"

"Is that English?"

"Sort of."

"Ya gonna go?"

"Got no choice. One good thing came of it though. I'm getting special computer lessons at home. With Miss Adonia. First lesson's tomorrow."

"Ya call that good? I thought ya hated homework."

"That's not homework. Computers are *meant* to be used at home."

VII

"Would you like a coffee, Miss Adonia?" Seb's mother asked, hovering at the study door. Seb and his teacher had been in there an hour.

"Yes, that would be lovely, thank you. And please, just call me Adonia. My last name's a bit of a mouthful for kids, I'm afraid, so I go by my first name."

Mrs Taylor smiled. "Would you like a biscuit with coffee…Adonia?"

"No thanks, we're just about finished here. I'll be leaving soon."

Seb studied the screen. Exhilarated. In one lesson he had learnt more than Mr Roberts taught all year. It was a two way flow though. Miss Adonia knew a lot, but Seb was able to teach her a few things too.

Miss Adonia stood and stretched and picked up a magazine that was lying on the desk.

She smiled. "Star Trek. Bit of a Trekkie are you?"

"Yep. Even got a costume."

"Let me guess. Spock?"

"Close. Another Vulcan. Tuvok."

"Logical unemotional men. You relate to them, do you?"

"They make sense."

Miss Adonia laughed. "All Vulcans have Asperger's."

"Have what?"

Miss Adonia stared at Seb. "You don't know what Asperger's Syndrome is?"

"Never heard of it."

Miss Adonia was quiet. Seb went back to the work on the computer.

"Milk? Sugar?" Seb's mother asked, coming in with a tray.

"Black, thank you."

"It's very kind of you to give Seb these lessons. We'll pay you of course."

"No need. The school's policy is to extend children wherever possible. The sports teachers' after hours coaching is built into their contracts. Taking advanced lessons is built into mine. With computers, it's easier for the child to learn on his own equipment, so we travel."

"Mr Roberts never did that."

"No. It's just being trialed. Mr Roberts will be back soon, did you know? Maybe by the end of next week."

"Mr Roberts is coming back?" Mrs Taylor glanced at Seb. She knew what he thought of the old man.

Seb scowled. Life was unfair. The first decent teacher he'd had in years and she was going.

"If you like I could continue Seb's lessons…for a while." Miss Adonia offered. "It's nice to have such a bright student."

"Yes please," said Seb and Mrs Taylor nodded gratefully.

"DID YOU ENJOY your computer lesson, son?" Seb's dad asked over dinner that night.

"It was great!"

"I'd enjoy computer lessons if I had a teacher who looked like that."

"Like what?"

"Come on Seb. You're not blind. I mean that young and pretty."

Seb said nothing. He had not noticed. How she looked was not important.

"Have you done your homework?"

"Not yet."

"You've got to do it, Seb. It's important."

Seb's mother lowered her head. Don't start, she said in her mind to her husband. Not now when he's happy. Leave him be.

"I'll help you later, Seb," she said out loud.

"He shouldn't need help. He's big enough to do his own homework."

No one said anything.

They all knew the script.

And dinner time had to end with uncomfortable silence.

Chapter 5

The Invitation

I

"I'm giving Seb one last chance," Kristie said. "What would you think if I invited him out to the movies on Saturday?"

"Tomorrow? Your first date! Go for it, chicky babe," Jen laughed.

Kristie blushed. "What I mean is, let's get a group together. Ask Madeline maybe. I quite like her. And Guzzle. He's Seb's friend."

"Guzzle! You've got to be kidding! He'd never lower himself to be seen with us. I heard he's going out with Kaziah."

"Really? ...no that couldn't be true."

"Why not? He's a sporting hunk and she's a groupie. They suit each other."

"I bet Seb doesn't know. He'd flip."

"He'll find out soon enough," Jen said.

"AND THEN AFTER the movie we could go out for pizza. What do you think?" Kristie asked.

Seb sat stiff, not knowing where to put his hands.

They sat at one of the picnic tables scattered under the trees in the schoolground. Kristie, Jen, Madeline and Seb.

"I don't like pizza."

"Don't like pizza! Everybody likes pizza!"

"I don't therefore *everybody* can't."

"Oh well, we could go to Lucky Joes then. Whatever. Do you want to come?"

Seb hesitated. He wished Guzzle was here. He'd know what to do. He'd have the right grin. The right words.

He looked at Kristie. Looked straight at her face for the first time. As if he could find his answer there.

"You have beautiful blue eyes," he said surprised, "like a clear blue sky with wispy clouds."

Kristie choked.

Jen laughed, "How original."

"He's right," Madeline said. "That's just how they look."

"So that means you'll come to the movies?" Jen asked.

"What movie is it?"

"I don't know. Haven't decided yet," Kristie said, trying to brazen out the fact her face was bright red.

"I'll go if it's science fiction."

Kristie scrunched up her nose.

"I like sci fi," Madeline said.

"Well I don't!" Jen said. "Besides I don't think there are any sci fi movies out at the moment."

"I won't come then," Seb said, getting to his feet. "Thank you for asking me," he added politely. Like a little child being prompted by his mother.

II

"Who the hell do you think you are!" Jen yelled at Seb in the library.

"Shhh, we'll be sent out," Seb said.

"I don't care. Why did you treat Kristie like that? She's only trying to be your friend!"

What did she mean? Treat Kristie like what?

Seb's blank look said everything.

"You don't understand, do you? You don't realise how much you've hurt her."

"I never meant to hurt her." Seb's voice quavered. "She's nice. I like her."

"Well you've got a funny way of showing it. First telling her how pretty her eyes are and then knocking her flat."

"I didn't hit her!"

"I mean not coming to the movies with us, idiot!"

"I'm not an idiot."

"Well stop acting like one then. It's no wonder you've got no friends if that's how you treat people."

Jen headed for the door, then stopped. "And if you ever want to speak to Kristie again the first thing you say had better be, 'sorry'."

Sorry?

Sorry for what?

Seb ran the whole conversation at the table over and over in his mind. He did nothing wrong.

Just told the truth.

There's nothing wrong with that, is there?

"Seb."

He looked up. Madeline stood in front of him. What now?

"When Kristie asked you to come with us to the movies, she was really asking if you'd be her friend," Madeline said softly. "The movies are unimportant. They're just a reason to be together."

Movies means friends.

He'd said no to movies, therefore he'd said no to friends. How was he supposed to realize that?

"I thought you should know." Madeline said.

"What do I do now?"

"Come to the movies. Say you'd love to go, and say sorry you were rude."

"But I don't like the movies. And I wasn't rude."

Madeline shrugged. "Go to the movies to please Kristie. Or not go and lose her friendship. Your choice. And Seb, you *were* rude. Sometimes truth is not the best policy."

THE DAY WAS nearly over. A time of half light and long shadows.

"You have to speed this up, Adonia. It's taking too long," Rodin said leaning against the deck rails.

"It's not that easy. You've forbidden me to deal with this openly and we still don't know if he is who we are after."

Rodin searched her face. "You're not getting soft on me now, are you?"

"He's just a kid. We can't afford to make a mistake, for his sake."

"And you can't afford not to do your job…for your sake."

Adonia glanced up to reply, but Rodin had already gone inside. Slid in with the shadows.

She rubbed her arms against the evening chill. Thinking.

III

"I tell ya, the old guy's like a weasel. He moves quick and silent. Bit of a creep, I think." Guzzle lolled on Seb's bed watching Seb destroy a devilish creature on his computer.

VICTORIOUS flashed on the screen.

Seb saved his game.

"How did you see this, anyway? Are you spying on Miss Adonia?"

"Hardly. I was just under the bridge with…with some friends and glanced up at the right moment. I told ya you could see her place from there."

Seb turned back to the computer and logged on to the net.

"Look at this," he said. "I found it last night."

Guzzle leaned over Seb's shoulder.

"Asp…?"

"Asperger's Syndrome."

"Is that a new game?"

"No, read a bit more."

"Ya know I'm hopeless at readin'. Tell me."

"It's autism."

"I've heard about that. Aren't they those people who stare at walls all day, rockin'?"

"The extreme form can be like that."

"What about it?"

"I think I've got it."

"What! You're nothing like that."

"Asperger's is on the mild end. I did a check list. Ticked 22 out of 24 traits."

"Like what?"

Seb scrolled down. "See there," he said, "People with Asperger's Syndrome don't relate to others; can't understand gestures and the different tones in speech; may find sport confusing; lack of empathy; don't follow latest crazes. They often have a high pain threshold; can get caught up on one subject; follow rigid routines; don't like change; can have a high sensory perception, like finding certain noises irritating. May like to wear the same clothes each day, usually loose, non clingy items. It even mentions hating homework."

"Shit. Does sound like ya."

"It's not all bad. It also points out the traits of honesty, reliability and a genius streak in many areas, such as science, maths and computers."

"Well that's certainly you. It's not catchin', is it?"

"No. I was born with it. It's neurological."

"It's what?"

"A problem with my brain. Wired differently."

"What are ya gonna do?"

"Can't do much at all. It's how I am."

"Shit mate. I'm sorry."

"Sorry for what?"

"That you've got Asp…"

"Asperger's Syndrome. Why would that make you sorry?"

"Well it's not exactly normal, is it."

"It's normal for me."

"So ya're not worried? Ya don't mind havin' it?"

Seb thought a while. "I'd like to understand people better, but I don't really care about the other bits. If I didn't have Asperger's than I wouldn't be so brilliant at computers."

"Obviously being humble is not part of this syndrome thing," Guzzle laughed. "So are ya gonna tell ya parents?"

"Yes, and Miss Adonia. I think she knows anyway. She mentioned it last week."

"Did she? I don't think ya'd better tell anyone else though. Least not the kids at school."

"Why not?"

"They might tease ya and stuff."

"They already tease me."

"No need to give them more ammunition."

"I guess not."

IV

"You want to go to the movies? With whom?" Mrs Story asked.

"Kristie, Jen, a couple of others maybe."

"Any boys?"

"Perhaps."

"You can't go if boys are going."

"Mother!"

"You're too young for the dating game."

"I'm not dating anyone. I just want to go to the pictures with my friends."

"Friends! Huh! Why would you want a friend? You can't trust anyone, Madeline, and don't you forget it. Those you call friends one day, backstab you the next. You're better off on your own."

"All alone. Is that what you want? You want me to be lonely and resentful and hate the world for the rest of my life? Like you? What's wrong , Mother? Why are you so bitter?"

Mrs Story stared at her daughter. "I knew that sleepover was a bad idea," she said finally. "Twenty four hours in some slut's house and all your values fly out the window."

"Kristie's not a slut! You've never even met her."

"I don't need to. I can see the influence she has over you. One day with her is all it took for you to get boy crazy."

"That is so untrue…!"

"I don't want you seeing her again. You're grounded."

"Oh really? And what does that mean? I have to stay in this house and not go out. I'm banned from watching any show on TV that might give me enjoyment. I can't have friends over. Wow Mother, that's a tough punishment…oh wait, no it's not. That's how I've lived every day of my life. Permanent grounding."

"Sarcasm is cheap, Madeline." Mrs Story began to walk from the room. Discussion over.

The fight went out of Madeline. Fear set in. She would pay for this outburst.

"I just want to go to the movies," Madeline whispered.

Chapter 6

Movies

I

Seb shuffled in his seat. The movie was so boring. Pointless. The main character, a woman with a hideous laugh, was mistaken for a rich widow. Everyone else in the film was a moron who ignored the obvious.

Seb glanced at Kristie. She was laughing. Caught his eye and grinned. Seb smiled back. A quick stretching of the mouth.

He'd gone back to Kristie that day she asked him out. Apologised. Sort of. It's hard to say sorry when you don't know what you've done wrong. Anyway, she accepted the gesture and now there were six of them watching the stupid show. Was this a real date? Seb wasn't sure. After all Kristie had asked him out. He only knew Jen and Kristie. Madeline wasn't here. Pity. The others ignored him, just as he ignored them.

The sound track was very loud. Occasionally Seb put his hand over his ears and rubbed them to block out the noise. Didn't notice the raised eyebrows and smirks around him. The smell of the buttery popcorn made him feel queasy. He shut his eyes, but the onslaught on his senses continued. He held the arm rests hard enough that the screws underneath cut into his skin. The pain grounded him to reality.

"You OK?" Kristie mouthed.

Seb nodded. Kristie reached for his hand. Linked her fingers between his. Knuckle to knuckle.

Seb froze. Is this what it meant to hold hands? Someone else's body invading his? Kristie smiled at him shyly. Her knuckles ground against his skin.

How could she like that?

Seb breathed deep. Felt a familiar panic. His stomach muscles cramped. Eyes blurred.

He clenched his fists, catching Kristie's fingers in his grip.

"Ouch, you're hurting me," Kristie hissed. Seb let go and lurched to his feet.

"Sit down in front!"

"Move, you creep!"

"Seb, what's wrong?"

The girl on the screen screeched with laughter.

Seb stumbled out of the theatre. Trampling on feet, bumping shoulders, spilling people's popcorn and coke. He didn't hear the shouts of protest. Didn't hear the insults and abuse. Crashed through the lines waiting in the foyer. Staggered to the eatery area. Couldn't breathe.

He headed for a coffee shop. Had eaten there once before. Knew the booths at the back were dark and quiet. A hole. A cave. A sanctuary.

Seb fell onto the upholstery covered seat and held his hands over his head on the table.

II

"Hello, Seb."

Seb didn't look up, but he recognised Miss Adonia's voice.

"I bought you some tea. Camomile. It helps settle the nerves."

He heard the chink of the saucer on the table.

"Is it OK if I stay, or would you prefer me to go away?"

"You can stay," Seb said. His voice was muffled against his arm.

"I was shopping and I saw you running. A panic attack?"

Seb nodded.

"Happen often?"

Seb shrugged.

"What set it off?"

"The movies."

"Haven't you ever been to the movies before?"

"Yes, but Kristie chose this movie."

"Ahh," Miss Adonia sighed, understanding. "So you went to please her? It was out of your control."

"Madeline said I had to go, to be Kristie's friend." Seb sat up and wiped his eyes. "Now she'll hate me."

"Not if you explain why you ran away. Friends listen to each other."

"I'm not talking to her again. I couldn't."

"Try writing. Does she have e-mail?"

"Don't know. Am I like this because of Asperger's Syndrome?"

Miss Adonia looked at him warily.

"I did a search on the computer. I've got it, haven't I?"

"I'm not a specialist, Seb, so I can't diagnose you. But I suspect you do."

"How do you know about it?"

Miss Adonia hesitated. "My brother has it. Sort of runs in my family a bit."

"Can you help me?" Seb took a cautious sip of the tea. The flavour was strange, but not unpleasant.

"I am. I'm giving you computer lessons."

"I mean with understanding people and things like that."

"Maybe we could talk about things while we're programming. But you have to tell your parents. They need to know and you will have to see a doctor to get it confirmed."

"Dad will freak. He already thinks I'm wacko."

"You're not wacko, Seb. Just different. And you might be surprised. He might be pleased to know there is a reason for what you do."

"Maybe."

Miss Adonia watched the boy drink. Saw him slowly relax. Decided that Rodin was wrong. To be fair to Seb, she had to be upfront. "Seb," she said hesitantly, "there's something I have to ask you."

"What?"

"Seb? Are you OK? We've been looking everywhere for you." Kristie and Jen came up to the booth nervously, not knowing what to expect. Seb put his head back on the table.

"Hello, Miss Adonia."

"Hello girls. Seb is fine now. But it would be good if you could stay a while. Talk to him."

"No," Seb said getting to his feet. "I'm going. Sorry I spoiled your movie, Kristie." And they watched helplessly as he walked away, shoulders bowed. Then he stopped and turned and said to Miss Adonia. "Could you explain it to them? Please?"

Miss Adonia nodded and Seb shuffled off into the crowd.

III

Kristie lay on her bed and stared at the ceiling. She tried to imagine what it would be like to be Seb.

To be constantly confused by everyday things.

To misunderstand the simplest jokes and the most obvious sarcasm.

To fail to recognise the difference between a friendly gesture and one of threat.

Imagine feeling pain when you held hands because senses were too refined. Going crazy because lights flickered for you alone.

Kristie tried to understand.

But failed.

MADELINE LAY ON her bed and stared at the ceiling. She wondered how the movie went. Wondered if the group went to Lucky Joes after and chatted about the story line over milkshakes and doughnuts. Laughing and joking and enjoying themselves.

Mother's punishment started today.

Silent treatment.

She was good at that.

An expert.

Didn't cook Madeline's dinner. Sat at a table set for one and ate a ham and cheese omelette. Madeline's favourite.

Did not acknowledge her hesitant 'hello'. Did not speak at all.

Madeline, the ultimate invisible person. She felt her skin ripple as if it were fading away. As if she could look in a mirror and see her heart pump slower.

She made herself a sandwich then sat at her computer and logged into the chat room. Friends she had that her mother knew nothing about. With eyes blurred with tears she typed "Calling Mr Minty."

GUZZLE SHARED THE last of his beer with Kaziah. They were down at the park. A big group tonight. Ten, maybe more. One kid was smoking cones through a cut up coke bottle. Kaz breathed deep on a joint, but Guzzle stuck to his cigs.

"What ya wanna do tonight?" Dan slurred.

"Hit the school?" a girl said. Her hair was full of grass seed and twigs.

"Nah. They doubled security since last time."

"Let's just walk a bit. See what's happening."

They rose as one. Mindless. Led by boredom and artificial highs. A swarm without a queen. Kicked over bins. Trashed letterboxes.

And Guzzle stood and stared at the stars as Kaz threw up in someone's garden.

SEB SPENT THE night on the computer. Searched the web aimlessly. He heard Miss Adonia's voice in his head. "There's something I have to ask you."

Wondered what it was.

IV

"Sit with us, Seb," Kristie called when she saw him heading under the buildings.

Seb hesitated. Today was Guzzle's free day. No footy training. They usually ate lunch together, but there was no sign of him anywhere.

"How are you feeling?" Jen asked as he settled beside them.

"OK."

"Have you told your parents about 'it' yet?"

"About Asperger's? I told them last night."

"Wow, that would have been hard," Kristie sighed.

"No it wasn't. I just told them." Seb sipped on his chocolate milk.

"How did they take it?"

"What do you mean?"

"Were they upset?"

"Why would they be upset? Having a name for what I am doesn't change anything."

Kristie stared at him. "Yes it does, Seb. If I found out I was autistic I don't think I could bear it."

"That's because you don't have it. If you did have it, you'd still be the same person you were before you found out."

"So your parents were cool about it then?" Jen asked.

Seb shrugged. "Dad didn't say anything. Mum was crying after dinner, but she said she was OK when I asked her what was wrong."

"Seb! If your mum was crying that means she was upset, probably about your Asperger's."

"But she said she was OK."

"And you believed her?"

"Yes."

"And what did you do then? Walk away?"

"Yes. I had some research to do."

Jen and Kristie looked at each other. "Your poor mother," Kristie said.

"What did I do wrong?" Seb asked.

"People don't cry because they are OK, Seb. She was hurting. You could have given her a hug or something."

"Hug? I never hug my mum."

"Well you could have sat and talked to her then."

"About what?"

"You just don't get it, do you?" Kristie tried to explain. "You think your parents aren't upset about you having Asperger's, but they probably are. Your dad went all quiet and your mum cried."

"But there's no reason to get upset. I'm still the same person."

"The same person with a life sentence."

"I'm not dying."

"So you don't mind having Asperger's?" Jen asked.

"Why should I? Some of the most brilliant minds in history are suspected of having it. Mozart. Einstein."

"Really? So you might be famous one day?"

"It's great that you have a genius streak, Seb," Kristie said. "Everyone knew that anyway. But what about the other stuff. It's not exactly normal to get panic attacks from watching a movie, or," she blushed, "from holding hands."

Seb shrugged. "What's normal? Is Dan normal? Chalk? I don't want to be like them. Maybe I'm the normal one and everyone else is weird."

"Watch out. Barbarella's on the war path," said Jen suddenly as their headmaster rounded the corner. They watched as he ordered a group of kids to pick up papers.

Seb frowned. "He's not at war."

Kristie laughed. "Do you always do that? Think so literally?"

"Yes."

"You must have been very confused when you were little. What did you do when someone said 'Hop to it'?"

"I hopped."

"What about when you were being silly and someone said to 'grow up'."

"I stood on my tip toes."

Kristie and Jen giggled.

"How about when you were told to 'pull your socks up'?" Jen asked

"I pulled them up."

"What about, 'I'll be there in a minute'?"

"I timed a minute."

"That's amazing!" Kristie laughed. "English is full of sayings like those."

"Get lost," Jen chuckled.

"Have a chair."

"Take a break."

"Go jump."

"Run away, little boy."

"What about newer sayings," Kristie said really warming to the topic. "A computer byte!"

"RAM space on the computer!" Jen cried. "It makes me sheepish just to think of it!"

"That reminds me," Seb said. "Kristie, have you bought your new computer yet? There's a new PC just come out. Double the RAM of what you have now."

Kristie and Jen looked at each other. "Oh gosh is that the time!" Kristie cried. "Choir practice, Jen. Sorry, Seb. We've gotta fly. Catch you tomorrow."

And Seb sat alone with visions of girls with wings and huge butterfly nets.

Chapter 7

Grandma

I

When Madeline arrived home from school she found a row of suitcases standing at the front door. They were her cases, girlish pink. Almost unused. Bought for a rare holiday years ago.

She felt sick inside. What was going on?

"Oh Madeline. You're home." Mrs Story came into the room. Her eyes were red and she sank on to a couch, dabbing her tears with a hanky.

"Mother?" Madeline said, not game to move. Obviously the silent treatment was over, but that did not mean the punishment was.

"Terrible news."

Madeline did not speak. Her stomach crunched with tension. That was a common phrase in this house.

Terrible news. Your toys had mould on them. I had to throw them all in the bin.

Terrible news. I dropped your birthday cake. Can't eat it off the floor now, can we?

Terrible news. You've been so bad Santa's not coming this year.

"Grandma's dead."

It took a moment for the words to sink in.

"Grandma?

"Heart attack. Very sudden."

Madeline slumped. Sat on the edge of a suitcase.

Grandma. Grandma who tried hard to make Madeline's life bearable. Who used to pamper her when Mother wasn't watching. Who cuddled and hugged and told Madeline she was beautiful.

Grandma. Mother's mum. Whom Mother had fought with again and again until she'd finally left town dragging Madeline with her.

Grandma. The voice at the end of the pay phone, reverse charges, who listened and gave advice and sent kisses through the wires.

Gone.

"The funeral's in two days. I'm flying out tonight. Probably won't be back for a week. I'll have to organise her affairs."

"You're going without me?" Madeline's voice was full of tears. "I want to go too."

"Why would you want to come? It's a funeral, not a party."

"I want to…say goodbye."

"You'll only get in the way."

"Please, Mother."

"For goodness sakes. What a morbid child you are. Fancy begging to go to a funeral. Anyway you'll be happy. I've organised for you to stay with the Spencers. Talk girl talk with that Kristie."

Talk girl talk, when Grandma's just died?

Madeline looked at her mother almost in awe. The punishment was perfect. If she didn't know better, Madeline would have believed that Mum committed matricide just to hurt her.

Mother knew how close she and Grandma were. Knew how devastated Madeline would be. Knew that forbidding her to go to the funeral would be one more blow.

Then in the midst of Madeline's grief, Mother gave her the one thing she wanted most, freedom to be with friends, knowing the week would be forever tainted with sorrow.

II

"Guzzle said you can see her motel room from here. It must be that one," Seb said pointing. "It's the only one with a deck facing this way."

He, Kristie, Jen and Madeline were walking under the bridge on their way home after school. They stopped and looked.

"Guzzle said she lives with an old man that moves like a weasel."

"So why is someone like her living with an old man in a hotel," Kristie asked.

Seb shrugged. "Could be her dad."

"Maybe they're lovers," Jen said slyly. "Maybe she's his sex slave!"

"Jen! That's gross."

Seb looked faintly sick. Surely that couldn't be true.

"Maybe he's *her* sex slave!" Jen laughed loudly at the thought. "She seems to be a lady who likes to be in control."

"What does that mean?" Seb asked.

"Haven't you noticed her in class, the way she watches everyone so closely? Mr Roberts never even walked around to see if we did any work."

"There's nothing wrong with that. She's the best teacher I've ever had," Seb said.

"I know what you mean, Jen," Kristie said. "She seems just a bit *too* interested in what we do, and she looks so young it feels weird for her to be our teacher."

Seb frowned. "What's age got to do with it?"

"It's not just that. It's other things as well. Like her memory. She read the roll once and hasn't forgotten one kid's name."

"I've got a good memory. I knew every train station to the city by the time I was three."

"Go on," Jen said. "Say them."

"FernyGrove–Keperra–Grovely–OxfordPark–Mitch elton–Gaythorne–Enoggera–Alderley–Newmarket–Wi lston–Windsor–BowenHills–BrunswickStreet– Central. Then on from there it's…"

"OK, OK I believe you!"

"And I know all your phone numbers."

"How come?"

"From the school directory."

"Do you know every number in the directory!"

"Only the ones I've looked up."

"Yeah, well, you're creepy too," Kristie said with a smile.

Seb frowned and looked away. Was she being mean or friendly?

"Hey look. There's Miss Adonia now," Jen said.

They watched their teacher lean on the deck rail of her unit. Her hair was loose and long.

"She got home fast," Jen said. "Must have missed her lover."

"You're sick, Jen," Kristie said

"She probably just doesn't like the other teachers. Don't blame her," Seb said. "I wish she was staying though instead of Mr Roberts coming back."

"When will that be?" Kristie asked.

"Next week I think."

"Bummer," Jen said.

"But I thought you didn't like Miss Adonia much," Seb asked confused.

"Even a sex mad, femme fatale, girl genius, control freak is better than Mr Roberts," Jen said flippantly.

Kristie burst out laughing and Seb shook his head. He'd never understand girls.

They walked on. Past the debris of teenage boredom. Past the TWS scrawled on the pylon.

Madeline had not said a word. Hands hung limp at her sides. Eyes dull. Hair uncombed. Fading, fading away. The weight of her books in the bag on her back felt good. A tangible burden to counteract the many invisible ones.

III

"Tell me about your grandma."

Madeline glanced at the clock. 11.33pm.

"How did you know I was awake?"

"You've been tossing for ages. I'm not used to sharing a room," Kristie said.

"Sorry."

"It's OK. The funeral was today wasn't it?"

Madeline nodded in the dark.

"What was she like?"

Madeline thought a while. How to put Grandma in words? "Plump," she said finally. "With saggy skin and the softest face you've ever felt. All round and smooth. And when you cuddled her, you put your arms around this huge waist and you felt as if there was something solid in your life."

"You were close?"

"Very. I haven't seen her for years though. She and Mother had a fight. Mother ripped up every letter Grandma sent me. Not that I saw her do it. I just saw the bits in the bin."

Kristie was silent.

"I rang her though. Often. From the school pay phone. Reverse charges. Couldn't do it at home. The phone bills are checked carefully. And we e-mailed. Mother has no interest in computers, so it was safe."

"Do you have a picture?"

Madeline reached under her pillow and drew out a plastic wallet that held a bus pass. She slid a picture out from under the ticket and handed it to Kristie. "It's my only one."

Grandma and a much younger Madeline. The paper was creased and ragged.

"She looks just like a grandma should."

"Yeah." Madeline's eyes filled with tears.

"I've got an idea," Kristie said. "Come with me."

The girls tiptoed in their pyjamas to the study and shut the door. Kristie started up the computer.

"What…"

"Shh. Wait."

Madeline's eyes were drawn to a huge pin board covered in family snap shots, ballet ribbons and certificates of music, soccer pennants and movie memorabilia. A life in mosaic. A happy life.

She turned and her grandmother's face smiled at her from the computer screen.

"You scanned it!" Tears stung.

With a swirl of the cursor, Kristie wiped away the crease marks and cleaned the background.

"There. Do you want a border?" She tabbed down a selection.

In wonder, Madeline pointed to a rich curled design. Elaborate and old fashioned. With a click Grandma was framed.

"Now to print it." Kristie chose 2 copies and pressed OK. The printer whirred to life and Grandma's picture slid out from the tray.

"Here," Kristie said giving the first one to Madeline. Madeline held it with tender hands.

She stroked the paper cheeks with longing.

"Grandma," she whispered.

IV

Kristie picked up the second print, then hustled Madeline out of the study into the kitchen. She picked up a candle and picnic mat from a shelf.

"Come on. We're not finished yet."

She led the way outside. The moon shone bright.

Madeline followed, dazed. Picture to her chest.

Kristie nodded to a pair of gardening shears on a window ledge. "Take those and cut some flowers," she said.

"Kristie, …it's late."

"The best time."

In a dream Madeline snipped blossoms and fern spray, uniform midnight grey.

Kristie lit the candle and placed it in the middle of the mat. With care she folded and creased Grandma's picture into the shape of a heart. Madeline lay her picture beside the candle and sprinkled it with flowers. An altar. In memory.

"Tonight," Kristie whispered, "We lay Grandma to rest. Loved and never forgotten."

She handed Madeline the heart. "Tear it up," she said, "into tiny pieces."

"But…"

"Trust me. And when you do, remember your good times together."

Madeline shut her eyes.

"For candy canes at Christmas." She ripped the heart in half.

"For kisses and hugs."

Another rip.

"For remembering I was a real person."

"For never forgetting my birthday."

"For listening."

A sob tore from her throat. Ugly gasps of sorrow. "For loving me for who I am," she choked.

The pain was too much. Tears flooded down her cheeks. Wet and hot.

"Grandma, I want you back!"

"She hasn't gone, Madeline," Kristie whispered. "Look, she's all around you." Kristie picked up some of the paper and tossed it into the air. It fluttered on the breeze.

Madeline stood up, her hands cupped with memories.

"I love you Grandma!" she cried tossing the fragments to the wind. She spun beneath them, face to the sky.

Candle flicker.

Paper flutter.

Heart healing.

Moonshine memorial.

For Grandma.

Chapter 8

People From the Inside

I

"Seb's one of the girls now," Dan sneered, as he came up to the picnic table. "Do you enjoy your little chats together?"

"Go away, Dan. Get a life," Jen said.

"I bet you have a real *gay* time."

"I'm not gay," Seb said between closed teeth. Head down.

"What! Are they your girlfriends then?" Dan said.

"Yes," Seb said.

Chalk choked on his coke and sneezed it through his nose. "You! You have three girlfriends?"

"He meant we're just friends, now get lost, Chalk," Kristie demanded.

Dan sidled up to Jen. "I'm good at girly talk too. Come and sit on my lap and we'll chat about the first thing that pops up."

"Creep," Jen said.

"Hey, chocolate milk." Chalk grabbed Seb's drink from the table. "Good for growing bones. Does mummy make you drink your milk every day?"

"Give it back." Seb grabbed wildly and missed.

Chalk aimed the opening at Seb. "You want it, do you?"

"Yes!" Seb yelled.

"Leave him, Chalk."

Chalk looked up. Guzzle stared down at him. A head taller and twice his weight.

"We were only mucking about. Want a drink?"

Guzzle took the carton and gave it to Seb.

"Hey, Guzzle," Dan said. "Great night last night. Not that you'd remember much, I bet. Kaz said you were rolling drunk."

Seb stiffened, staring at the ground.

"We're going down to the shed. Coming?" Dan continued.

The shed. Where kids smoked, and teachers avoided duty.

Guzzle stood still. Frozen with indecision. Felt a hand slip into his. Long fingernails grazed his palm.

"Come on, Guzzle," Kaz said.

He turned and allowed Kaz to lead him away.

Did not look back.

There was a stillness at the table.

"You didn't know about him and Kaz?" Jen said finally.

"No," Seb said.

More silence. Then...

"Why would he want to go out with her?"

Kristie shrugged. "She's beautiful. Popular. They look good together."

"She's not beautiful," Seb said. "You're beautiful. She's mean and ugly."

Kristie blushed.

"You see people from the inside, Seb," Madeline said softly.

The others stared at her. She was so quiet they'd forgotten she was there.

"Dan and Chalk break the rules all the time. How can he stand being with them? I thought he was *my* friend."

"He is, or he wouldn't have stuck up for you just then," Jen said.

"I don't understand," Seb said, standing up and throwing his unfinished drink in the bin.

II

He walked through the school buildings alone.

Betrayed.

Lost.

Left the girls behind without a word.

Thumped the walls as he went.

Rhythmically.

In beat to his anger.

Pounded through those in his way. Didn't even see them.

Thump and thump and thump and thump.

Kaz

and

Guzzle

and

Chalk

and

Dan.

Why?

Why ... everything?

Thump and thump and thump and thump.

Why would Guzzle choose such friends?

How could he stand touching that girl? Fingers entwined. Didn't it hurt him?

Getting drunk. Losing senses. Killing brain cells. Why did that make you popular?

It was

all

so

stupid.

Thump!

A window smashed.

Glass shattered.

Blood dripped.

Girls screamed.

Seb stared stupidly at his hand and felt no pain.

III

"Adonia? Oh, I'm sorry, I should have called you. I don't think Seb's up to a lesson this afternoon." Seb's mother wrung her hands at the front door.

"I heard he hurt himself. Is he OK?"

"Twelve stitches, he needed." Mrs Taylor's voice broke. "And we have to pay for the window."

"May I come in?" Miss Adonia asked gently.

"Of course. Where are my manners? Would you like a coffee?" Seb's mother was shaking as she led the way down the hall.

"Thank you, but sit down Mrs Taylor, I'll make it. Just point me in the right direction."

Mrs Taylor waved erratically at a cupboard.

Miss Adonia put the water on to boil.

"I don't know what to do," Mrs Taylor sobbed suddenly. "He's on a two week suspension…at least. The school is talking about expelling him."

"What did he do?"

Mrs Taylor blew her nose on a tissue. "I'm not exactly sure. Apparently he was walking along hitting the walls. He does that at home all the time…thumps things…seems to need it. I've tried to stop him. I bought him a punching bag and even strapped a mattress up once, but he never used them. He likes hard things. Cupboards, walls." She glanced up at the crockery stand. "No Thumping Zone," was taped across the glass. "Anyway they said he hit a couple of kids and then smashed a window with his bare fist."

Miss Adonia sighed in sympathy. "And before that?" she asked.

"What?"

"What upset him in the first place?"

"Oh goodness knows. Someone sat in his seat in class. They ran out of chocolate milk at the cafeteria. He's lost his way to class…he still does that you know after all this time. It could have been anything."

"Did anyone try to find out?"

"Seb refused to talk."

The kettle screamed and Miss Adonia made coffee.

"I don't know what to do any more."

"Has Seb talked to you at all about the possibility he has…" Miss Adonia paused.

"Asperger's Syndrome," Mrs Taylor finished the sentence. "Yes, he mentioned it."

"And?"

"It's possible. I don't want to think about that right now."

"If he does have it, it would explain his behaviour. The school may reconsider his expulsion."

"You think?"

"I'm sure."

Mrs Taylor sipped her coffee. Her eyes were glazed and still.

"You never think it can happen to you. I wanted a baby so much and when he was born and I held this gorgeous squirming bundle, I thought he was the most beautiful thing in the world. Ten fingers. Ten toes. But they don't count brain cells, do they. Then he screamed and tantrumed his way through his early years. It was as if a little alien I couldn't understand and had no way of communicating with had invaded my world. And now he's all grown up and I still don't know my own son."

Miss Adonia leaned over and patted Seb's mother's hand. "Seb is a wonderful bright boy. Believe me, if brain cells could be counted, he'd win prizes. It's just that they're put together in a different order. It doesn't make him less of a person."

"He doesn't sleep much, you know. No more than five hours a night. Never has. Imagine having a baby that whines and cries all day, goes to bed at 10 at night and wakes at 3am. You have no idea how hard that was. I thought I'd go crazy with sleep deprivation until I realised that he didn't want me around anyway. We got him a computer when he was three. I felt like I was the worst parent in the world for allowing him so much unsupervised screen time, but it was that or I'd go mental. Do you understand? No of course you don't, how could you. Nobody knew what was wrong and I did what I could to stay sane. Besides, it made him happy and there weren't many things that did. Maybe if I'd spent more time with him. Tried harder, things would be different."

"It's OK, Mrs Taylor. You did what was right at the time. Don't punish yourself for being a caring mother," Miss Adonia said.

Mrs Taylor grabbed a handful of tissues and blew her nose. "He's such a difficult kid, but he's *my son*." she sobbed. "My only child. I love him so much. It kills me to see him so unhappy."

"Then learn to see things from his eyes for a change. He's had to adapt his way of thinking to yours since the day he was born."

"What will I tell his father?"

"The truth of course. I'm sure your husband is an intelligent man. Give him facts then give him time to come to terms with things. And you'd best get Seb diagnosed as soon as you can. It can take months to see a specialist and you'll need to take concrete evidence to school."

"They may withdraw the threat of expulsion, but he's still suspended for two weeks. Exams are coming up. What if he fails? It would drive him crazy to repeat a year."

Miss Adonia stared at her cup. "I could tutor him if you like." she said. "Just for the two weeks. In the mornings maybe, set him tasks for the afternoon. I could start next Monday."

"You'd do that? What about your job?"

"It's just about finished. Mr Roberts returns next week."

"Well, …that would be wonderful…" Hope shone in her eyes. "I don't know what to say. Are you sure?"

"Yes."

"But why would you bother?"

"Seb is an exceptional student. Therefore exceptions must be made for him."

IV

"How's the hand?" Miss Adonia asked sitting next to Seb at the computer.

He held up a heavily bandaged palm. "I made sure they left my fingers free so I could still type."

Seb's mum hovered at the doorway. "Seb, Miss Adonia has agreed to tutor you until your suspension is over," she said. "Is that OK?"

"Yes!"

"That's settled then." She left, shoulders a little lower, face more relaxed. They listened to her footsteps fade away.

"What happened today, Seb?"

"Got upset. Broke a window."

"Upset? About what?"

"Had a fight with Dan and Chalk…and Guzzle."

"Did you tell anyone?"

"No."

"Why not? You might not have got into so much trouble."

"Rule number one. Don't tell."

"Who told you that?"

"Everyone knows that. If you tell, you get it worse the next day. Anyway, I don't care. I'm glad I'm suspended. I hate school."

"I understand. But if your parents explain to your teachers that you have Asperger's then people might be a bit more understanding. And besides, if you are going to be a world famous computer specialist, you need to finish your schooling."

Seb shrugged. "I suppose."

"And so you can sit your exams in a few weeks, we'll start your lessons tomorrow. We won't worry about them now. You've had enough to deal with today. Let's have a bit of a surf instead." She swivelled the keyboard towards her and typed rapidly. The screen flickered and changed as the computer obeyed the commands. Finally she tapped the last key and an emblem filled the screen. A scroll enveloped an octopus whose tentacles waved to and fro around a box that said, "Please enter security code."

"Ever seen that?" she asked.

Seb nodded. He was vaguely aware of his mother's voice calling, "Down the end of the hall, girls, he'll be glad to see you."

He barely glanced up when Kristie, Madeline and Jen entered his room.

Didn't acknowledge their hellos.

"Cute little octopus," Kristie said. "What site is that?"

"It's…" Seb began.

"It's Octoplus," said Jen.

They all looked at her.

"You know, the new merger between Platinum and Computerworks. That cute little octopus will soon be on most of the software you'll buy."

"I didn't know you knew about computers," Seb said to Jen.

"I've got three brothers who are computer geeks. It's hard not to pick up some things. They think this latest system is amazing. It's a program that guarantees secure data transmission between Octoplus supported programs and servers."

Kristie screwed up her face. "Is that English?" she asked.

"Why are you looking up Octoplus?" Madeline asked.

"Don't know," Seb said. He looked at Miss Adonia. "Why are we?"

"Just general research," she said. "Now that your friends are here, we'll leave it for another day."

V

"I tell you, Jen knew about Octoplus. We could have been wrong all along," Miss Adonia said as she paced the room.

"Knowing about a major computer company is nothing special. Did you access her student profile?" Rodin asked.

"She's new. Only this year's grades were on file. The ultimate Miss Ordinary. Rarely misses school. Punctual. Polite. Friendly. She's so average that it's almost abnormal. Got straight B's last report. Every subject. Not one B+ or B-. Only B's."

"Even computer studies?"

"Yes, but that means nothing." Miss Adonia stood at the window and stared at the park in the distance. Some kids were tagging the bridge walls, oblivious to passers-by who ignored them and hurried past. "It's possible she knows more than she's letting on."

"A straight B student could not have done what we suspect has been done."

"The person we are seeking is bright enough to rig her own results."

"We already know Seb can do that. Think what you're saying, Adonia. If this Jen is covering her tracks, why would she have revealed herself now? It doesn't make sense."

Miss Adonia sighed. "I guess you're right. I'll keep working with Seb. But I have to be honest. I don't think he's the one. He's too...naive."

Rodin raised his eyebrows. "This is the same kid who's just been suspended for smashing a window with his bare hands?"

"I know it sounds strange, but he's not the violent type. He's simply misunderstood," Adonia insisted.

"Misunderstood people can do unexpected things."

Adonia sighed again, "I guess you're right."

SEB TURNED ON the air conditioner. When he was younger his mum drew cartoon characters around the dial to show the temperature level. Seb selected the Snowman.

The temperature plummeted as he curled up tight in his sleeping bag.

Never used sheets and blankets. Too messy, too hard to keep on the mattress.

In his sleeping bag he was in his sanctuary. A refuge.

A retreat from the assault of the world upon his senses.

A world of squeezy comfort.

Never slept without it even in the hottest weather, which was why his parents installed the air conditioner.

But they needn't have bothered. Seb didn't feel hot or cold much.

He thought about his day.

Guzzle's betrayal.

Slashed hand.

The release from school for a fortnight.

Lessons with Miss Adonia.

They churned in his mind.

Couldn't sleep…again.

So many nights spent with restless thoughts and worn out body.

Seb visualised his brain. Named the cortices, each spinal thread. With imagined shears he sliced the strand of consciousness and finally drifted to sleep.

GUZZLE LAY IN his bed with a pillow over his head.

But he could still hear Angus in the next room.

Like a putrid stink, the sounds would not go away.

He tried to blur the words so none could be understood, so they became a backdrop like thunderous rain or a loud TV show. Meaningless drone.

But some still penetrated.

"…filthy bitch…

…useless…

…deserve this…"

smash

crash

bash

and when the silence came, Guzzle crept from his room and held his mother long into the night.

Chapter 9

Violation

I

Rodin rose early. Checked his computer. There were 20 e-mails, but the encrypted mail caught his eye. Made a strong coffee while he thought.

"Anything?" Miss Adonia asked, orange juice in hand.

"I got some new information from the office. There has definitely been a large amount of overseas flow to and from this school over the years. I think it's time to see Seb."

Adonia paused. "I'll see him today for his lessons, but I just can't imagine that it's him. He doesn't seem the type."

"What exactly does a cracker seem like?"

Adonia shrugged. "I've had access to his computer, yet I found nothing out of the ordinary."

"It would all be well hidden. He's hardly likely to have shortcuts on the desktop." Rodin sipped from his coffee. "We need to delve deeper. Face him with what we know then see what happens. I'll come with you to his lessons this morning."

Miss Adonia paused. "I don't think that's a good idea, Rodin. Seb likes routine. Even having me there is new for him. Let me handle this."

"There's no time for pussyfooting it, Adonia. I'm coming. Arrange it please." He turned to the screen again and kept working.

Miss Adonia stared hard at his back, but he did not acknowledge her. She sighed and went to telephone Seb.

SEB EYED THE man on the doorstep with Miss Adonia uneasily. He didn't like surprises.

"Hello, Seb. Hello Mrs Taylor," Miss Adonia said. "I'm sorry to do this with so little warning, but this is Rodin, the man I told you about. He's a specialist in programming and would like to see Seb's work."

"Of course that's fine," said Mrs Taylor opening the door. "Seb's been looking forward to you coming."

Seb led the way to the study; joy gone from the morning. Instead of free and easy lessons with a teacher he trusted, a stranger entered his life. Someone he had to talk to and make the effort to get to know. An effort he did not want to make.

But Rodin did not attempt small talk. He wandered around and studied the row of Seb's dad's books on the shelves. He fingered a glass paper weight and frowned. Seb relaxed as the computer clicked to life and Miss Adonia took her usual place beside him.

"This is a very clean room," Rodin said suddenly.

Miss Adonia glared at him.

"Where's all your stuff, Seb. A computer buff like you must have heaps of games and things. Maybe more computers?" His voice was deep and soft and made Seb nervous all over again.

"I've got two computers, that work."

"Where's your other one?"

"This one is Dad's. Both of mine are in my room."

II

"Of course it's all right to use Seb's computers if Seb doesn't mind," Mrs Taylor said when Miss Adonia called her back to ask permission. "But is it really necessary? His room is a bit of a mess. He likes to be alone in there, don't you Seb. If I try to clean it, he gets upset when I move things."

"We won't look at the mess, Mrs Taylor. But we do need to use his computers. They have more…facilities than your husband's."

"Seb?" Mrs Taylor asked.

"OK," he replied sullenly.

Seb's room was more like a spare parts storage room than bedroom. A cannibalised computer was strewn across a huge desk. Hard drives and motherboards lay amongst CDs and old keyboards. Games and programs filled the shelves on the wall.

Mrs Taylor gave the sleeping bag on the bed a quick shake and smoothed it flat. Kicking shoes and socks and books and manuals to one side she made room for two more chairs.

"Tea? Coffee?" she asked.

"No thank you. We'll be fine," said Miss Adonia.

With a quick smile, Seb's mother left the room.

"Interesting hardware," Rodin said, examining the computer. "Who showed you how to put a rig like this together?"

"Worked it out myself. Read books. Read stuff on the web."

"Stuff? Like what? Could you show me what you have?"

Seb tabbed to the main menu.

"Is that all?" Rodin asked. "It's not much, is it?"

"I don't keep a lot on the local hard drive," Seb said, "just a few programs I use all the time. I like to have a lot of free space."

Rodin scanned the screen as it scrolled down. Nothing unusual.

"What's on your other drives?"

"One for programs and one for research."

"Can I take a look at your programs?"

Seb opened a drawer and selected a hard black case. He powered down and inserted it into the computer then rebooted.

Rodin frowned. "These programs here? What are they? I don't recognise them."

"I wrote them," Seb said. "Want to see one?"

As he opened a source file Rodin's eyes widened in surprise. "What language is this?"

"Just a scripting language I wrote myself."

"Seb," Miss Adonia said, "this is incredible work!"

Seb nodded.

"Have you released this online? There are people who would be interested in this," Rodin asked.

"No. I was just mucking around."

Rodin regained his composure. "Do you have any recent programs like the new one Octoplus released last week?"

"No. I don't need it. Couldn't afford it anyway."

"Wouldn't you be tempted to just go in and get it and see if you can crack it?"

"That's illegal."

"People still do it though."

"I'd never do that. Dad's really strict about computer stuff. He won't let me burn my friends' games."

Rodin leaned close to Seb. Too close. Seb backed away.

"A boy as clever as you could easily hide it from his dad, couldn't he? Could put it on one of your hard drives and tuck it away out of sight. No one would ever know."

"What would be the point of that? Why have a program and not use it?" Seb said nervously. He didn't understand this man.

"Seb," Miss Adonia said quietly, "There are some people who crack programs just because they can. They do it as a challenge. Many never use the programs they steal. They just boast about them on the net and swap the programs they have with others who crack."

"That's stupid. If they're so clever, why don't they create their own stuff? I design programs, not steal them."

"Some people crack to give a company warning that the security codes aren't tight enough," Rodin said. "They see themselves as good guys. They don't do it for money and they have a weird moral code that forbids them from sharing their knowledge. It's a bit like them saying, 'I can steal your program, so you'd better tighten security or others will steal it too'. Maybe that's more your style, son."

"I'm not your son."

"Last week on day zero, the Octoplus system was cracked."

"Day zero?"

"The first day it was released."

"How do you know that? Who are you?"

"I guess you could call us Internet detectives. Our job is to prevent and intercept Internet crime."

"Both of you?" Seb asked, looking at Miss Adonia. "You're not a teacher?"

"Well I am, but I've branched into net security."

"So you're only here because you think I crack software." Seb hurt inside. Betrayed again, by someone he trusted. "Why do you think it was me?"

Miss Adonia sighed. "We had certain leads we had to follow."

"Leads?"

"We managed to trace the attack to a service provider in this area. We think it was routed through your school's system. Isn't that coincidental, considering your skills and your access to the school computers?" Rodin inquired.

"I didn't do it," Seb insisted, jumping up. "You can check if you like. Look through my drives. You won't find anything."

"Don't mind if I do," Rodin said and he sat at the computer and began typing. He was fast and knew what he was doing. The screen flickered in response.

Seb lay on the bed, wrapped the sleeping bag around his body and hid from the accusations.

Miss Adonia stood frozen with indecision. She knew better than to touch Seb, to try to give comfort, but it all seemed so wrong…so unnecessary.

"Wait," Miss Adonia said.

Rodin ignored her.

"Seb's telling the truth. We were wrong. He's not who we are after."

"We'll know soon," Rodin replied, not taking his eyes from the computer.

"We know now. We should go, Rodin. We have done enough damage as it is."

"Sit down, Adonia."

Miss Adonia bit her lip and turned to Seb and spoke to the rumpled bag. "Seb. I'm sorry. So sorry. But we have to check you out, don't you see. It's our job and you were so talented that we thought you were the one we sought."

Seb said nothing. And Miss Adonia sat listening to the tap and click of keys as they violated Seb's trust.

III

Seb and Guzzle sat under the bridge throwing pebbles at beer cans rusting in the water.

Guzzle skipped school.

Too tired to concentrate. Anus beat his mum up again last night. Had finally settled her into his own bed at 3am, a bag of frozen peas at her cheek to dull the bruising.

Fell asleep on the floor beside her.

Seb had no school to go to.

Told Miss Adonia not to come back for tutoring either.

Left his mum in tears begging him to change his mind.

Exams loomed.

An axe above their heads.

"I'm pissing outta here," Guzzle said suddenly.

"What?"

"I'm leaving."

"Huh?"

"I can't take it any more."

"Can't take what?"

"Anus beat the shit outta mum last night. I wish she'd leave him. But she won't. Says she still loves him. Makes no freakin' sense."

"You can't just leave. Where would you go? "

"Who cares. Anywhere's better than here."

Seb tried to imagine walking into the unknown. Shuddered at the thought of nameless cities and indefinite destinations. He needed to *know*. Needed routine and familiarity.

"What about Kaziah? She's your girlfriend, isn't she?"

Guzzle shrugged. "Sort of. She's pretty, and easy. Bit of a bitch at times."

Seb knew the bitch part. "What's 'easy'?" he asked.

"Shit mate, sometimes you're such a kid. She lets me touch her, you know, do things."

Seb gulped. Desire and repulsion in one.

"Have you done *it*? All the way?"

"Nah, not yet. Close but. She's OK, but not enough to stay for. Besides, her friends are morons: smoke dope and beat up anything they can get their hands on. I'm sick of 'em."

"What about exams?"

Guzzle rolled his eyes. "Ya gunna change my grades again, 'cause that'll be the only way I'll pass?"

"If you want."

"Nah. Thanks anyway. Thought I'd leave tomorrow night. Anus starts night shift at the factory. Sleeps all day. Probably won't miss me til the weekend. I'll be long gone by then."

Tomorrow. The word started to sink into Seb's brain. A date. A real time. This was not just talk. Guzzle was going. His only true friend was walking out of his life.

"Don't...go," Seb said. "I don't want you to."

"Come with me then."

"I can't."

"Don't blame you. I wouldn't leave if I had it good like you either."

Seb thought of his life. Suspension from school. A father who barely talked to him. A mother who cried all the time and who had never understood him. He was a perpetual victim. And, of course, now his Asperger's.

"What's so good about my life?"

"Ya gotta nice house. A dad who doesn't beat up ya mum. Parents who buy you whatever ya want. Geez, how many computers you got now? We don't even have a TV that hasn't had a fist through it. And you're a freakin' genius. You'll probably be the next Bill Gates and be rollin' in money before you're twenty. I'll be the bum in the street your Rolls almost ran over."

Seb grunted. "And I've always wished I was like you. Popular. Girls fall all over you. You know how to talk to people without making a fool of yourself. Never thought you envied me."

"Don't envy ya ugly face though."

Seb grunted. "We should merge," he said. "Blend all our molecules in an atomiser and come out as one. With your body and my brain we could take on the world."

"Yeah, well, when ya invent this machine, come and find me. I'll be in a gutter somewhere."

Seb stared at the refuse stagnating in the mud.

"Don't go," he said again.

"I gotta," said Guzzle.

IV

"Madeline," Kristie's mum said as the girls walked in after school. "Your mother sent me a letter. She asked if you could stay here for another week. I thought I'd talk to you before I rang her. Would you like to stay here? You're welcome to, of course." And it was true. Madeline was quiet, polite and helpful. A perfect guest.

"Thank you. I'd like to stay," Madeline said.

"Good, well that's settled then." Kristie's mum handed over a piece of folded paper. "She put this in the envelope for you. I'll go and phone her now. Would you like to talk to her?"

"No."

Madeline waited until she was in her room before opening the note.

Dear Madeline,

I'm having a lovely time. I've caught up on heaps of relatives and laughed over old times. Alistair came over from New Zealand. Grandma's will is a bit more complex than I thought it would be. I'll be stuck here a little longer. Hope you don't mind.

Wish you were here,

Love Mummy.

"I hate her," Madeline said.

"Your mother? What's she done now?" Kristie asked, removing her school shoes and wriggling hot red feet.

Madeline tossed the note on the bed and Kristie read it.

"Her own mother has just died and she's *having a lovely time.*" Madeline's voice broke. "She forbids me to go to the funeral, and now has the audacity to write ... *wish you were here.* And as for the *Love Mummy* bit, that's just plain bizarre. I've never called her Mummy and I can't remember the last time that she told me she loves me. I don't know where she got her sadistic talent from, but she's damn good at it."

Kristie said nothing. Her mum couldn't have been more different. She had no experience of emotional cruelty.

"Who's Alistair?" she asked finally.

"My uncle. Mother's brother. I think I've seen him twice in my life. Mother hates him even more than she hates…hated Grandma. They haven't spoken in twenty years."

"She seems happy enough to see him now," Kristie said.

"Huh. Only if she can use him in some way."

"Do you have any other aunts and uncles?"

"No. But Alistair's married, so I guess I inherited an aunt and I've probably got some cousins I've never met."

"What about your dad's side," Kristie asked cautiously. She'd never heard Maddy speak of her father.

Madeline shrugged. "I don't know who he is. Mother won't say. To my knowledge I've never met him. He may not even know I exist. That would be just like her, to hide my existence from someone who might have cared."

Kristie couldn't begin to imagine a life like Maddy's.

"I want to go home," Madeline said suddenly.

"I thought you wanted to stay here?"

"I do, I just need to check on things. Water my plants. Get the mail. Stuff like that."

Be by myself.

Cry alone.

"I'll ask Mum to drive you."

"No thanks. I want to walk."

V

Madeline opened the door and stood at the threshold of her house looking in. It was so clean. Sterile. She'd never realised that before. Had a stranger stood where she stood, there would be no way to guess that a teenage girl lived here.

Kristie's home was cluttered with photos and knick knacks, certificates tacked to the wall, the fridge hidden under notes and lists and novelty magnets. Her existence reaffirmed on every surface of her home. Here, Madeline didn't exist.

Madeline wandered through her house seeing it with new eyes. Nothing was out of place. Every book in the book case was perfectly in line. Not that there were many, her mother read magazines mostly, and even those were stacked meticulously. In the cupboard, the wine glasses stood at attention beside the good crockery set that had never been used. Not once.

Madeline walked down the hall and stopped at her mother's bedroom. She was not allowed in there. It was Mother's place, the only room with a catch on the inside, to keep Madeline out. She remembered times when her mother would lock herself in the room and not come out for days. When she was very young there were times Madeline had lived on breakfast cereal, the only meal she knew how to make for herself.

But the room was not locked now.

She opened the door.

It was neat and tidy. The lone thing that showed personality was the collection of shoes. Pretty ceramic shoes, jewel encrusted shoes, soft velvet ones and others made of pewter, all in wooden display shelves. Rows and rows of them along one wall. Magical things to a little girl, but Madeline was forbidden to touch them. Indeed had rarely seen them.

She picked one up. It was cold and hard. Like holding her mother's heart. She put it back, resisting the urge to smash it on the ground.

Left the room.

Closed the door.

Went and turned on the computer.

Grandma always made sure Madeline had an up to date machine. Saw how it was the only thing in Madeline's life that interacted without criticism. Let her into worlds that were not ruled by emotional manipulation.

This computer came last Christmas. One gift that could not be ripped up. Mother demanded it be put in Madeline's room, out of sight, with the volume off, as if that were a punishment.

Madeline turned it on and checked her mail.

Chapter 10

A Life Worth Living

I

Seb was watching TV when Kristie, Madeline and Jen were ushered in by a smiling Mrs Taylor.

"Some visitors," she said brightly. "Isn't that nice, Seb."

Seb did not look up.

A lady on the TV won a vacuum cleaner and she jumped around the stage hugging the host and kissing everyone in sight.

Mrs Taylor laughed nervously. "Well, I'll leave you kids to yourselves. Would you like a drink, girls?"

"No thanks. We'll be fine," Kristie said.

"Hi Seb," Jen said, sitting beside him. "I love this show. I watch it every afternoon. That lady's been on three days in a row now."

"It's a stupid show," Seb said.

"Oh," Jen said, taken aback. "Why are you watching it then?"

"Got nothing better to do."

"How's the hand?" Kristie asked, changing the topic.

"Fine." He did not take his eyes off the screen.

They all watched in silence.

"How are the lessons with Miss Adonia going?" Kristie said finally.

"They're not."

"What?"

"She thought I was a thief. I never want to see her again."

"A thief? You? That's crazy. You're so honest it's pathetic. I remember when once you found a pencil in the school yard and handed it in to the office."

"Tell that to her."

"What did she think you stole?" Madeline asked.

"Software. From the web. She's an Internet detective."

"She's a what!" Kristie cried.

"An Internet detective. Tracks down people who pirate stuff online."

"Why did she think you were doing that?" Madeline asked.

"Something was diverted through the school's computer system. She just presumed it was me."

"How did she know that? Did she find that out when she was our teacher for those few weeks, or did she become our teacher because she already knew it?" Kristie wondered.

"Doesn't matter," Seb said. "They're gone now and I hope I never see them again."

"Them?"

"Miss Adonia and that man she was with. Rodin."

"Rodent?" asked Kristie.

Seb smiled for the first time. "Rodin," he corrected her, "But rodent describes him well enough. He was just like a rat sniffing around my programs."

"Does your mum know all this?" Madeline asked.

"No."

"Are you going to tell her?" said Kristie.

"No," said Seb, "No point," and there was silence again as they watched the lady on the TV win another useless household item.

II

"So we got the wrong kid, that doesn't mean we were on the wrong track completely." Rodin watched Adonia pack her papers into a briefcase.

"I should have trusted my instincts all along," Miss Adonia replied clicking the case shut. "The crack was too sophisticated and achieved too quickly for a kid his age, and Seb showed no signs of guilt or wariness. I don't think it has anything to do with this place. It was simply a decoy, and we fell for it."

"I'm not so sure," Rodin said. "There are a growing number of extremely brilliant computer literate kids out there. After all, you're not *that* much older than Seb is. It wouldn't surprise me at all that one could pull this off."

"We've burnt our bridges. I'm no longer employed at the school."

"No need. I have full access to their computers now."

"Good for you."

"Internet theft is a major criminal activity. It's not nice. You can't get all squeamish just because you feel an attachment for the accused."

"I'm not squeamish," Miss Adonia insisted. "Sure I liked Seb, but if he'd cracked Octoplus he would now be in police custody. What I don't like is the way you accused him without proof, dragging me into your accusations. He's a sensitive kid, with enough problems of his own without being called a liar and a thief by a teacher he trusted."

"Come on, Adonia. You're an Internet detective, not a bloody child psychologist. So we got it wrong. Wouldn't be the first time a lead went astray."

"I know. See you at work next week so we can backtrack and find the real thief."

"You could stay until the weekend," Rodin suggested. "Relax a bit."

Miss Adonia flinched. "Goodbye, Rodin," she said firmly.

MISS ADONIA SAW Guzzle as soon as she entered the bus terminal. Knew that he was Seb's friend, but didn't know his name. She bought a coffee in a cheap plastic cup, then breathed deep and walked up to him.

"Hello."

Guzzle looked up at the voice.

"Mind if I sit here?" She gestured to the empty seat next to him.

Guzzle shrugged, fingering the ticket in his pocket...the most expensive one he could afford, that took him as far away as possible. The bus left in twenty minutes and then he'd be free.

"I'm sorry. I don't know your name, but I recognise your face from school. I used to teach there."

"Guzzle," said Guzzle.

"I'm..."

"I know who you are."

Miss Adonia frowned at the bitterness in his voice. She took a sip of coffee to steady herself. "Shouldn't you be at school," she asked, then hated herself for her patronising tone.

Guzzle shrugged again.

"You're Seb's friend, aren't you. I've seen you together."

Guzzle nodded, barely.

"Is he OK?" Miss Adonia asked. "He's had a rough time lately."

"Who's fault's that?" Guzzle snapped. "Seb's a freakin' genius and now he's gunna fail the year 'cause his tutor called him a thief and ran out on him."

Miss Adonia winced. "It's not quite like that," she began.

"Whatever," Guzzle said getting to his feet. "Listen lady, Seb's good. He's decent and honest and didn't deserve the crap dealt him. Now you're leaving and he'll fail. Simple."

"There's more to it…" she said to his back.

Guzzle didn't stop.

"Guzzle!" she called so he couldn't help but hear. "Maybe Seb doesn't deserve to have his friend walk out on him either."

Miss Adonia sat a while and thought. Her ticket read 'Non refundable" so she scrunched it into a ball and threw it in the bin.

Rodin was on his computer when she opened the door of the motel room. He raised his eyebrows and smiled. "Miss me?" he asked.

"Unfinished business," she said as she closed the bedroom door behind her.

III

"What does this program do?" Madeline asked. She had gone round to Seb's place alone that afternoon. Kristie was fast losing her desire to spend time with a boy who rarely acknowledged her and only spoke about computers and science fiction when he did. She and Jen went to Lucky Joes but Madeline wasn't in the mood for chit chat. Her own home was like a mausoleum, cold and hard and lifeless, and Kristie's place was too full of sympathy and glances of pity. At Seb's she could be at peace.

"It searches for key words on the web. When the key word is found on another site it goes in and copies the information then collates it in a file."

"That's amazing. And you designed this?"

Seb nodded.

"What information are you gathering?"

"At the moment I'm researching DNA. I'm sure there's a way to alter our molecular structure to improve life span. There are some obscure companies around doing fascinating research into this area. When they post their info, my program brings it to me."

"Isn't that stealing their knowledge," Madeline said without thinking. Saw the hurt on Seb's face and wished the words away.

"It's not illegal. All the sites are available to anyone. My program just makes the searching automatic."

"I didn't mean..." Madeline began.

"You think I did it, don't you," he said staring at the screen. "You think I cracked the Octoplus system."

"I don't think that..."

"It's because I'm different. Different doesn't mean untrustworthy, you know."

"Seb," Madeline said forcefully. "Listen to me. I don't believe that you cracked the program. It's way too complex."

Seb looked at Madeline. As she stared back at his pale grey eyes, she realised that this was the first time they had ever had eye to eye contact. His intensity was unnerving.

"How do you know it's so complex?" he asked.

Madeline smiled weakly. "Because I tried to crack the program myself. Well, not *really* crack it," she added quickly, "I just went to look for a backdoor. There wasn't one."

Seb did not blink. Just stared.

"I just looked at the program from the outside," Madeline said defensively. "I was curious."

"You're the one who called me Mr Pimpernel on my computer at school, aren't you?" Seb said, finally looking away.

"Yes," Madeline said quietly.

"And put an appointment on Miss Adonia's personal schedule."

Madeline nodded. "Grandma taught me, would you believe. Not everything of course, but she trained me in basic computer skills when I was young, and after we came here I had nothing else to do with my time, but to browse the web. Mother likes it when I'm quiet and out of the way so I spend hours on it every night. Learnt a lot in chat rooms and sort of went from there."

"Do you know who cracked Octoplus?" Seb asked.

"No idea. But there are not many people who could do it so quickly, and they won't be found that easily."

"Can you program?" Seb asked.

"A little. Nothing like what you're doing."

"I've got a problem in one area. Want to help me?"

"Sure." Madeline smiled, but Seb was already tapping away at the keyboard. She waited patiently trying not to show how excited she was to meet someone who shared her passion for the computer.

"Are you online?" she asked suddenly.

"Yes. I have a 24 hour connection," Seb answered still searching for a particular file.

"But you're not using it are you? I mean what you're doing now is not online, is it?"

"No."

"See those lights there," Madeline pointed to a box sitting on his tower. "Are they supposed to be flashing then?"

Seb followed her gaze and froze. He knew his system well enough to know that the only reason for those lights was outside access.

Someone had gained access to his computer. And if someone could get in then there was a good chance that person had complete control over it.

IV

"You're over Seb now are you?" Jen asked dipping her fries into tomato sauce.

"I guess. I still like him, but it's hard to compete with a computer," Kristie said. She fingered the vibrant pink cup that had Lucky Joes written on the side.

"You could put a box over your head and paint on a screen. That would make him take notice," Jen laughed.

"I'll start practicing my computer noises now," Kristie giggled. "Twing! You have mail!"

"Madeline went to his place this afternoon. Do you mind?"

"Nah. She's nice, but very quiet. They make a good pair."

"So are you interested in anyone else?" Jen asked.

"I'm giving up boys. I want to concentrate on school work and do good works for charity in my spare time," Kristie said primly.

"Right. And I'm Mother Teresa," Jen said.

"What about you? If you could choose any available guy, who would it be?"

"Guzzle," Jen said immediately.

"Guzzle! Kaziah would kill you."

"No harm in looking from afar."

"Why him? He's as thick as a brick and drinks too much."

"That's not fair," Jen argued. "He has a troubled family life. With a bit of love and compassion I bet he's capable of great things."

"Are you going to let him know of your admiration?" Kristie asked.

"Not a chance. I'm not suicidal. Kaziah *would* kill me. But they won't last together, and when she drops him for the latest bod in a football jersey, I'll be waiting to give him a sympathetic ear."

"I bet that's not all you'll give him."

GUZZLE STARED OUT the window of the bus. Outside was clear and lovely, but for Guzzle the landscape went past in a blur of murky colour. He hadn't realised the trip would be so long. Twenty six hours and still going. But then perhaps that was for the best.

The further away the better.

His mum had simply nodded when he told her his plans. Gave him every cent she could find in the house. Private stashes his stepfather knew nothing about. Wasn't much. Enough for a week's rent and a bit of food.

He held her tight for a long time then turned and left.

Didn't look back.

His mind drifted. Only two regrets. Mum and Seb. Asked them both to come. Both said 'no'. He was strong. Healthy. Sixteen. Old enough to get a job. A brickie's apprentice maybe. Something outdoors. Might join a local footy team. Could even get paid to play if he was good enough. And he'd work hard. Wanted to work hard.

Wanted a life worth living.

Chapter 11

Naughty Boy

I

"Do you trust me?" Madeline asked, staring at the blinking light on Seb's modem.

"Trust you to do what?"

"I can contact somebody who can trace that leak."

"What? Who?"

"It's hard to explain. Do you mind if I at least try?"

Seb shrugged and moved to give her room. Her arm pressed against him as she began to type. He shuddered and pulled away. But not from repulsion. Definitely not that, but he was not sure exactly what to call the feeling that made an electric shock pleasant.

"You're in a chat room!" he said when he finally forced his attention back to the screen. "Who's Mr Minty?"

"Just a name. I've never met him…or her."

"Then why…"

"It's a long story, Seb. You know how I told you my Grandma made sure I always had a computer?"

Seb nodded.

"She showed me the chat rooms and introduced me to Mr Minty. 'Trust him and no one else' was all she would ever say. I wondered sometimes if he was actually Grandma all along, but he's still there, and...she isn't." Madeline's voice broke and Seb looked up to see if she was crying. She wasn't but her face was sad and Seb tried to remember the appropriate response to other people's sorrow.

Suddenly a reply came through and he forgot everything but the happenings before him.

Hello Madeline.

"That's coincidental isn't it?" Seb asked. "That he was online just when you called him."

"He usually is."

"He has to sleep sometime."

"I don't know how he does it either," Madeline said as she started to type out their problem to her cyber friend. "But just about every time, night or day, I have tried to contact him, he replies within fifteen minutes. And he knows *everything* about computers."

"That's strange," Seb said.

Madeline smiled. "I guess it is, but I think of him as my guardian angel. He's never let me down yet." She finished entering the gist of their problem.

Leave it with me.

"See, I told you," she said as she logged out.

"He cracked Octoplus!" Seb cried suddenly. "It must be him. He used your link with the school and routed it through there!"

Madeline cringed. "I thought of that too," she said in a small voice. "But we don't *know* that for sure, and even if he did, he must have a good reason. I can't imagine anyone who takes time to comfort frightened little girls could be a bad person."

Seb nodded. That sounded right to him. If someone was nice to you, then they were good. If they were not nice then they were bad. Obviously.

But something niggled at his brain. Cracking Octoplus was bad...wasn't it?

A noise at the bedroom door made them both look up. Seb's mother came in beaming with happiness. "The school just rang," she cried. "They've lifted your suspension. Apparently Miss Adonia pleaded your case and they've decided that the possibility of you having Asperger's Syndrome changes things. You can finish the year, Seb!"

"Great!" Madeline grinned.

Seb sat stunned. Miss Adonia was on his side? But she called him a thief. The lines between good and bad blurred. Seb shut his eyes, then with a huge effort, aware that Madeline was watching him, opened them again.

"OK," he said, and to hide his confusion, he turned back to the computer screen – a place where he could hide emotions and appear at ease.

II

Mr Minty's hands caressed the keyboard, feeling their way, pressing this key and that one. The screen was alive to his touch, digits and numbers, bytes, formed and dispersed, transformed into signals and pulsed their way through phone lines, surging along the electrical current.

Half life.

Half energy.

All force.

Seeking the source.

ADONIA OPENED THE door and stepped inside…to be faced with a furious Rodin.

"What have you done?" he cried.

Afraid, she moved to the other side of the table, out of his reach.

"What's wrong?" she asked in confusion.

"My computer has been wiped! Everything's gone," he spat. "You're the only one who had access."

"That's ridiculous," she said, keeping the table between them. Biding time. Trying to make sense of what she was hearing.

"I went out for an early dinner. Came back and my files were erased." Rodin's voice was stilted. Barely controlled.

"I went to the school!" Adonia defended herself. "I got Seb's suspension cancelled. I didn't touch your computer. Do you think I'd come back here if I did?"

"If it wasn't you, then…" Rodin did not finish the sentence. He grabbed fistfuls of his hair and sank onto a chair. Lowered his head onto the keyboard of his laptop.

The black screen came to life.

NAUGHTY BOY

Adonia stared at the words in incomprehension. A machine that is wiped has nothing on it at all. "Naughty boy?"

Rodin sat up with a start and snapped the laptop shut.

"What's going on, Rodin?"

He shook his head. Said nothing.

Then it dawned on her. "You've been traced." She laughed. "The great Internet detective was detected."

"Shut up."

"So much for getting the cracker on side. He wiped everything then spent the time to install enough of an operating system to leave you a message. Clever." She went to the kitchenette and flicked the switch of the electric jug, feigning self control in the mundane action. Stood at the bench as the water boiled.

"But why 'naughty boy'?"

"I said shut up," Rodin growled.

"What have you been up to Rodin? You're too smart to let this happen. Where did you slip?"

Rodin marched into his bedroom and slammed the door behind him.

Adonia raised her voice. "It doesn't make sense. How did someone get in?"

The jug whistled and she made coffee then went and stood outside his room.

"Maybe you hacked into somewhere and got traced. Am I right? But you would never have done that if you thought there was any risk."

The bangs and thumps inside sounded like someone packing in a hurry.

She paused. Thought a while.

"You haven't been doing a bit of your own cracking on the side, have you? Got someone mad at you?"

The door opened and Rodin came out. Face set. Bags in hand.

"Don't be a fool," he said. "You realise our entire project has been compromised."

"But you have backups don't you?"

"Of course I do. That's not the point. Whoever wiped my files would have copied them first. And the links to the main computer would have also been traced. The data integrity scan we will need to do could take weeks, and then every password, every code will have to be changed."

Adonia paled. She knew all that of course, but hadn't thought that far. "Who do you think did it?"

"That's what I intend to find out."

A horn beeped outside.

"My taxi," he said. "See you at work next week. Be early. We've got a lot to do."

Adonia watched through the curtains as he drove away.

Something was wrong. The message, 'Naughty Boy' didn't make sense. Rodin spent his life chasing 'naughty boys'. He was one of the good guys. A cyber good guy anyway. His personal life was something else.

Seb's face flashed before her. He was their latest investigation. Surely he had nothing to do with the wipe. Rodin could have tagged Seb's machine. He had the chance…but Seb simply didn't have the know how to trace the tag even if he knew it was there. Must be someone else then.

Adonia sighed. She'd never know. Would probably never be told even if Rodin found out. All that work ahead. What was the point? Someone in the US could route an attack on a South African server through Australia, then download its data to a German who lived in Hong Kong. Even if they found the culprit, prosecution was a legal nightmare.

She sipped her coffee. There must be more to life.

Teaching was good. Bright minds, some of them even eager to learn.

Could become a tutor.

It was worth thinking about.

Definitely worth thinking about.

III

Madeline walked into hell.

Her mother was back. Waiting. In Kristie's house.

Kristie sat at the kitchen table. Pale. Gave a weak smile as a greeting. Fear in her eyes. Fear for Madeline.

"Hello Mother."

"Get in the car."

No one said anything.

Earlier Kristie's mum had greeted Mrs Story cheerfully, explaining that Madeline was at Seb's house and should be home soon. But she was taken aback by the venom in the woman's face. She'd tried to explain that Madeline had done no wrong. Tried to justify her friendship with Seb. Would not tell Mrs Story where he lived. Made up excuses. But she spoke to deaf ears.

They sat then, without speaking

Waiting.

Mrs Story said nothing all the way home. That suited Madeline. She couldn't have spoken anyway. Sick with dread, not knowing what was coming.

What would her punishment be this time? Mother was so extraordinarily inventive.

When they stopped at their house...just a house, not a home, Mrs Story stepped out of the car quickly. Shut and central locked the doors. Walked inside.

Madeline sat petrified with indecision. A car lock was hardly going to prevent her from opening her door, but her mother's intentions were clear.

Stay there.

Madeline sat.

For two hours.

Long after it was dark.

Saw her mother eat dinner with the curtains conveniently open.

Didn't care…couldn't have eaten a thing anyway.

Nauseous with tension. Needed to pee.

Finally Mrs Story opened the front door and gave one quick nod. Madeline spilled from the car and threw up in the garden. Spewing fear.

She stumbled into the house. Went straight to the toilet. Mrs Story waited outside.

"Go to your room," she said, when Madeline emerged.

Madeline went.

Froze in dismay.

It had been gutted.

Everything gone but a mattress on the floor.

Her desk, her clothes, precious things. All gone.

The computer. Her only line to sanity. Gone.

Madeline fell to the floor with a moan.

"I told you…" Mrs Story said mildly. "No boys."

And as she closed the door, Madeline heard a new sound. The bolt of a lock sliding into place.

TAP TAP.

Tap Tap.

Madeline swam her way through the thick slime of sleep.

Tap Tap.

Forced one eye open. Saw her watch in the moonlight. 1am.

Tap Tap.

Focused on the window. What? Who?

Then her eyes flew open. Fear washed over her.

Seb! If her mother saw him, she was dead.

She rushed to the window. Nailed shut. She knew that. It was the first thing she had checked.

"GO AWAY!" she mouthed.

Seb peered beyond her. Shone a torch into her room. "NO!!!!" Madeline screeched silently. "GO! GO!!!"

"Are you OK?" she saw him whisper.

She nodded furiously.

He switched off the light and stood there looking at her. He pressed his hand to the glass and slowly she traced the outline with her fingertip. Then he left. Melted into the night.

Madeline let her tears run down the pane, her hand still on the glass.

Crying because somebody cared enough to ask if she was OK.

SEB TOSSED AND turned. Couldn't sleep. Didn't understand the emotions that coursed through him. After Madeline had left earlier that night, he realised that he missed her. Wanted her company. Rang Kristie's place. Heard the news.

Guzzle was right. Seb had it good. His parents would never treat him like Mrs Story treated Madeline. He couldn't even begin to comprehend why a mother would act like that. Mothers were good. They cared. 'Bad mother' was an oxymoron.

Seb got up and turned on his computer. Sat like stone while it booted up, then found the link to the chat room Madeline had visited, logged on, and typed "Calling Mr Minty."

IV

Seb sat alone at lunch. His hand was still bandaged. A beacon to attract whispers and snide comments.

"He's the one who…"

"Psycho."

"…beat up some kids…"

No Guzzle to stand by him, to deflect tormentors.

No Miss Adonia to make class interesting.

Compulsory counselling sessions three times a week – the price of a reduced suspension.

School sucks.

Just two more weeks until the end of the year. Just two more weeks. A mantra for survival.

"Hi Seb," Kristie and Jen sat beside him. They didn't seem to care he was social death.

"Heard from Madeline yet?"

"She's hardly going to call *me*," he said. "It's my fault she's being punished."

"It's not *your* fault her mother is mentally unbalanced. I can't believe Maddy's not at school. Why isn't someone checking up on her?" Jen said despairingly.

"We *tried*," Kristie told Seb, shuddering at the memory of Mrs Story's hard face. "'Madeline is unwell,' is all her mother said before slamming the door. Mum even rang the school and told them that she was worried, but there's nothing they can do…apparently. She was only absent on Friday and that was not enough of a concern to call in authorities, especially as Mrs Story simply claims Maddy is sick."

"What's the point of becoming an adult if you are still as helpless as a kid?" Jen grunted.

Seb bent down and retied his shoelaces. Shut his eyes tight. Guilt over his part in Madeline's plight consumed him. Stayed doubled over a long time, then got up and, ignoring the girls, headed for the library.

Kristie and Jen looked at each other. Jen raised one eyebrow. "Is it something we said?"

"I don't think he means to be rude. It's all part of his Asperger thing."

"I don't care what it is, he can learn can't he." She raised her voice. "Hey Seb."

He stopped. Turned.

"We were talking to you."

He nodded.

"It's rude to walk away in the middle of a conversation."

"I don't have anything else to say," he said. "I want to be alone."

"That's fine, Seb," Kristie explained. "Just tell us that first. That's what friends do. Tell each other things."

Seb gave a quick smile. "OK," he said. "I'm going to the library. I want to go on the computer."

"Fine," Jen said. "See you later."

They watched his shuffling walk all the way to the library.

"That guy has so much to learn," Jen said.

"Don't we all," Kristie said. "Remember being young. Everything was so simple back then."

"Dandelion chains."

"Rocking horses."

"Kittens before they became cats."

"Barbie dolls."

"Ken!!!"

"You haven't changed, Jen."

Jen laughed. "Thinking of hunks with great bodies. Have you seen Guzzle lately?"

SEB LOGGED ON to the library computer and checked his e-mail. Only one. A huge grin spread across his face.

Hi Seb,

Guess what. You wont believe this, but I got a job already! Can hardly believe it myself. Met a guy on the bus who needed a gofer on this construction site. You no, I go for this and go for that and he wanted me to start straight away. Get to ware a hard hat. Girls love me!

There's a Internet cafe just round form the site. I chatted up the waitress and she showed me how to e-mail you. Why didn't you tell me that computers have spell checks. I could have passed English if I new.

Some of the guys play in a footy club on the weekends and said I could join up.

Not sure where Ill live yet. I'm staying with the boss for a couple of days. There's another job going if your interested.

Say hi to me mum if you see her. Tell her Ill rite one day.

Guzzle.

Seb stared at the screen. Reading and rereading.

Wished he could fall in.

Turn himself into millions of molecules and swim through cyberspace to emerge in Guzzle's café and say Hi.

Chapter 12

Decisions

I

"Get dressed."

Madeline woke as a pair of jeans was flung onto her face.

"And have a shower. You stink."

Mrs Story left the room, but this time did not lock it.

Madeline got up slowly.

It had been three days.

Three days without washing. Without cleaning her teeth. Without brushing her hair. Toilet stops twice a day and that was the only time she'd been allowed out of her room. She'd contemplated running, pushing her mother aside on those rare outings, crashing open the front door, fleeing down the street dishevelled, shouting for help.

But couldn't.

Two weeks of freedom did not break a lifetime of habit, and Mrs Story's mental hold over her daughter was far stronger than any flimsy door.

Madeline tiptoed to the bathroom. Smelt eggs and bacon and her stomach growled in protest. For days she'd been fed bread and water.

Laughed when her mother first left it on the floor.

"That's not very original, Mother," she had whispered under her breath, so she wasn't heard.

Madeline put the shower on hot and strong. Let the surge of water wash away three days of horror. Three days in which she'd come to the realisation that there was something seriously wrong with her mother.

"Eat, then fix your room," Mrs Story said, when Madeline finally entered the kitchen.

"Your Uncle Alistair is coming this afternoon and I want you to be on your best behaviour."

MADELINE EYED THE man across the table curiously. Her uncle. Grandma's son.

He was big, tall, with a neat trimmed beard and thick hair, more grey than black. His eyes were creased with smile lines and he looked kind and wise. Madeline tried to imagine him and her mother playing together as children. Swinging on ropes, climbing trees, playing tag, opening Christmas presents under a decorated tree as a family. Wondered when they had fought; wondered why they hadn't spoken in twenty years; wondered why he was here now.

"How's school, Madeline?" he asked. His voice was deep and smooth.

"Fine, thank you."

"And what else do you do with yourself?"

Madeline frowned, not sure what he was asking.

"Hobbies? Sport? Ballet? My girls are always into dancing of some sort."

"Your girls?" Madeline deflected the question.

"Cassie and Beth, they're ten and twelve respectively and Toby is fifteen."

Three cousins. Three parts of her family she'd never met.

"Now you have money of your own, you must fly over and visit us," Alistair continued.

Money of her own?

"Madeline, go to your room," her mother snapped. Mrs Story had said little since her brother arrived. Sat twisting a napkin through her fingers. Napkins Madeline had never seen before today.

Alistair grunted at his sister. "I didn't think you'd told her."

Madeline half stood, poised between obedience and a yearning to know more.

"Sit down, Madeline," Alistair said.

She sat.

"Alistair. No." Mrs Story used her 'command' voice. One which was to be obeyed.

He ignored her.

"I presume you haven't seen the will."

Madeline shook her head.

Mrs Story's face contorted. Rage. Confusion. Fear?

Alistair smiled calmly. "Let's go for a drive, Madeline. Show me your town. Where you hang out with friends. Your favourite place to eat."

Madeline rose as if in a dream.

She was Rapunzel climbing from the tower. Sleeping Beauty waking from a curse.

And as her uncle held open the door of his hire car, Madeline stepped into a new life.

II

"You own your own house!" Jen choked on her drink. "You mean the one you live in now?" She grabbed a napkin and dabbed her face.

"No, Grandma's house. It will be rented out, and I'll get the rent. I also get her car, not that I can drive it yet, and enough money to put myself through University," Madeline smiled. "Grandma left me just about everything. Mother, Uncle Alistair and my cousins got a little bit of money each, and I got the rest."

Jen whistled through her teeth. "Way to go, chicky babe!"

"Wow," Kristie breathed. "I wish I had a grandma like that."

Madeline stared at Lucky Joe's chequered tablecloth. "I wish I had a grandma," she said.

Kristie hung her head. "I'm sorry. I didn't mean…"

"It's OK. I know what you meant."

"What's your uncle like?" Jen said changing topics.

"Nothing like Mother. He's alive and Mother just exists."

"Does he know how your mum treats you?" Jen asked.

"I told him everything. We talked for hours last night."

"That must have been one amazing conversation."

"He already knew a bit. Things that Grandma told him, but I hadn't told Grandma everything. I knew she'd worry too much."

"Why hadn't he contacted you before now?" Kristie said biting into a fry.

"Mother made it clear that I was her child and no one else was to interfere with my upbringing."

"What I can't believe is how two people from the same family can not talk for twenty years," Jen said.

Madeline shrugged. "It's all quite complex. He really liked her, you know, when they were young. She was his big sister and could do no wrong. It was only when he was old enough to compete with her that they fought."

"Was she like that with you too?" Kristie asked. "Nice when you were little?"

Madeline nodded. "We did have some good times together…as long as I did what she wanted."

Jen twirled a straw around in her drink. "What are you going to do now?"

"I'm not sure. Uncle Alistair invited me to go to New Zealand to live with his family."

"Are you tempted?" Jen asked.

Madeline grunted. "What do you think? He goes back in a week. I have to make up my mind by then."

The girls finished the last of the fries.

"How's your mother taking all this?" Kristie asked finally.

"She locked herself in her room. Won't come out."

III

Seb and Madeline sat under the bridge.

It had been raining, and the water ran faster than usual, washing away flotsam. Ebbs and flows cleansed stagnant pools.

They sat close. Shoulders touching. Seb threw pebbles into the flow.

"Are you leaving?" he asked finally.

Madeline sagged. Allowed her head to fall onto his shoulder.

"I don't know," she said in a small voice.

Seb tensed. He could smell her hair. Nice. Clean. Felt it against his cheek. Soft. His arm was on fire with the proximity of another person. He had never been so intimate with anyone…ever. Couldn't even remember his mum so close. He was torn between sheer pleasure and the desire to run.

But she demanded nothing from him. Was content to sit quietly.

He relaxed and did the bravest thing he'd ever done in his life. He allowed his head to rest against hers.

"Kristie's mum invited me to stay with them until I finish school. They've got a spare room they said I could use."

"Really!" he said, his neck rigid, not game to move lest he push her away. "Can you do that? Will your mother let you?"

"Uncle Alistair threatened to take her to court if she tried to prevent me leaving," she said.

"That's serious."

"It's sad. It didn't have to be this way. I would have been happy to stay with her if she'd just given me a bit of freedom, but it's total control or nothing with Mother."

The water gurgled and scurried. Traffic droned overhead.

"You know what?" Madeline said suddenly.

"What?"

"I think my Uncle is Mr Minty."

"Did he say so?"

"No, but last night when I went to bed, he gave me a packet of mints. For no reason. Just smiled this strange little smile."

"Why don't you ask him outright?"

"I don't want to. It's like investigating to see if Santa is real, or whether the Easter Bunny brings eggs. I used to believe those things you know. Mother wasn't always that bad. She thought I was cute when I believed in magical things."

"I contacted Mr Minty that night I came round to your window. I didn't know what else to do."

"You did that for me?" Madeline brought her head up and stared at Seb. He left his head crooked at an angle. Too self conscious to move.

"I wondered how he knew," she said. "I thought it was just coincidence. And it was because of you all along.

You are so sweet, Seb. Thank you." She leaned over and gave him a kiss on the cheek then snuggled up to his arm again.

Seb's eyes blurred with emotion. He lost focus and found it hard to breathe.

She kissed him.

No fuss.

No slobbery saliva.

No expectations that he do anything.

His first kiss.

Not quite up to Guzzle's standard. But this was better.

He wouldn't swap the world for that kiss.

IV

"Are you sure you're making the right decision?" Alistair asked. He stood by his car outside Kristie's house, ready to go.

Madeline smiled. "No. I'm not sure at all. But then I've never had much opportunity to make my own choices. It will have to do, for now."

"I'm only a phone call away."

"Or a chat room?"

Alistair paused. Saw the knowledge in her eyes and gave a quick grin.

"It was Mum's idea. Your Grandma that is. She wanted me to watch out for you but knew that your mother would never allow me near you. So I became Mr Minty."

Madeline shook her head in amazement. "All those years and I never knew. How did you get back to me so quickly every time I contacted you? I always wondered about that."

Alistair held up the beeper he kept on his belt. "'Mr Minty' was a trigger word on my computer. When my computer picked it up, it rang a warning chime at work. If I was close by I'd hear it, if not, my computer was monitored by colleagues who knew to contact me by beeper."

Madaline shook her head. "You went to all that trouble for me?"

Alistair looked a bit embarrassed. "Not really. In my line of work I had many warning chimes to check out, although Mr Minty was one of the more pleasurable calls."

Madaline smiled. "Why were you called 'Mr Minty'?"

"Actually you named me. You couldn't have been more than two. Mum...your Grandma was babysitting you when I came to visit. I gave you a mint and I'm afraid got labelled immediately. That was the last time I saw you, 'til now. I hope it won't be that long again." He held out his hands and she came to him hesitantly. He wrapped his arms around her and gave her a big hug.

Strength. Security. He was like Madeline had always imagined a father would be. Alistair got into the car and started the engine.

"Uncle Alistair," Madeline said suddenly, leaning on his window. Needing to know before he left. "Did you crack Octoplus?"

He sighed and rested his arm on the sill. "I work for Octoplus. It's my job to find loopholes in the security system and to track down anyone who manages to crack in once the programs are on the market. Sometimes we use outside cyber-security companies to help and we suspected that there was a rogue operator in one of them."

"Rodin?"

"Yes."

"And Miss Adonia?"

"As far as I'm aware she's innocent. She's just Rodin's assistant. Anyway we set a trap for him. I cracked Octoplus and he was sent on a trail of my making so we could track his methods of retrieval."

"Why did you route it through my school's system?"

Alistair shrugged. "I had the address. After all I've been there often enough. It's amazing how frequently Mr Minty got called during class time."

Madeline blushed. "Mr Roberts was boring. I had to do something creative or I would have gone insane."

"Anyway I knew Rodin was trouble when I caught him stealing Seb's program."

"Is that what he was doing?" Madeline exclaimed. "We knew he hacked into Seb's computer, but we just thought he was looking for the Octoplus system."

"No, Rodin was being a very naughty boy," Alistair said. "But I did get to see Seb's work. Very impressive. He's a clever young man. Tell him to contact me, when he's finished school. There's a job waiting for him, if he's interested. I believe he already has my address. Now I really have to go or I'll miss my flight. Keep well, Madeline. Visit soon."

"I will. Goodbye."

Madeline watched the road long after the car was out of sight.

After

Exams were over.

Seb stared at his results without expression. They were as he expected. A+ for computer studies and advanced maths. The rest of the subjects he passed, just, but they didn't matter. He handed his report to his mother. She smiled with relief. She gave him a quick hug and to her astonishment he returned the embrace. He held her too tight, as if he wasn't sure of the correct pressure involved in hugging, and he let go so fast she stumbled backwards, but she stared at him in wonderment.

"Thanks Mum," he said, the words awkard off his tongue. "For not giving up on me."

"You're welcome," she said, holding back tears of love that she knew he would misinterpret as sadness.

"I'm going over to see Maddy. Is that OK?"

"Fine," she said calmly, as she thought to herself, "That is so incredibly, wonderfully fine that I could scream."

"B'S AGAIN. FOR everything!" Jen exclaimed, sitting on the lounge in Kristie's house. "I could get into the Guinness Book of Records for the most predictable student."

"How about you, Maddy? What did you get?" Kristie asked.

"I did OK."

Kristie peered over her friend's shoulder and whistled. "How do you manage to get grades like that?"

"Up until recently I had little else to do with my time but study."

"But I notice that you've been a little preoccupied lately, chicky babe," Jen said suggestively. "And speaking of preoccupation…here he comes."

They watched Seb through the curtains, stroll down the garden path and knock on the door.

Madeline rose. "I'll be back later," she said.

"Be good little kiddies," Jen called. "Be home before dark."

THEY WALKED HAND in hand, not the knuckle twisting type of holding hands, but the palm to palm kind, curled together. Comfortable.

"I have something I want to show you," Seb said, but as they turned the next corner, Madeline stopped.

"This is the way to Mother's house."

"There's something you should see."

"I'm not ready to face her yet."

"Trust me."

Madeline felt sick inside. Gripped his hand so hard her fingernails left welts in his skin.

"I can't." She tugged him away.

"She's gone, Maddy."

"What?"

"Your mother has left."

Madeline allowed him to lead her to the place she had spent most of her life.

A 'FOR SALE' sign was hammered into the lawn.

One front curtain was ajar and Madeline peered into bare rooms and hollow space. Everything was gone. Cupboards, tables, chairs, books, the little teapot shaped like a house she was never allowed to touch. Gone.

It was like her past was erased. Only it wasn't of course. It lived on inside her. She shut her eyes and everything returned. Neat in its place.

She started to shake.

Seb put his arm around her, and held her awkwardly not knowing where to place his hands.

She buried her face in his shoulder and guided his arms around her back.

"That's how I need to be held, Seb. Just for a little while."

Her head fitted neatly under his chin and silent tears wet his shirt. They stood a long while together as Madeline listened to echoes of her past.

Then she spoke, her voice muffled against his chest, "Mother's gone but I'm glad you're here, Seb."

And Seb smiled and marvelled that, for just a moment, the haze was clear.

Other titles by *Kathy Hoopmann* for younger readers

Blue Bottle Mystery
An Asperger Adventure

Nothing is quite the same after Ben and his friend Andy find an old bottle in the school yard. What is the strange wisp of smoke that keeps following them around? What mysterious forces have been unleashed? Things become even more complicated when Ben is diagnosed with Asperger Syndrome.

ISBN 978 1 85302 978 3

Of Mice and Aliens
An Asperger Adventure

When Ben and Andy discover an alien crashed landed in the backyard they are faced with a problem. They want to help Zeke repair his ship, but why does he ask for such strange things. Can they trust him?

ISBN 978 1 84310 007 2

Lisa and the Lacemaker
An Asperger Adventure

Lisa's Great Aunt Hannah draws Lisa into the art of lace making and through the criss-crossing of threads, Lisa is helped to understand her Asperger Syndrome. But Great Aunt Hannah also has a secret and now it is up to Lisa to confront the mysterious Lacemaker and put the past to rest.

ISBN 978 1 84310 071 3

CPSIA information can be obtained at www.ICGtesting.com
Printed in the USA
LVOW010415270911

247892LV00001B/4/P